A Novel

Sandra R. Pound

outskirtspress
DENVER, COLORADO

Money
A Novel

v4.0

Outskirts Press, Inc.
http://www.outskirtspress.com

ISBN: 978-1-4787-4538-9

PRINTED IN THE UNITED STATES OF AMERICA

DEDICATION

This book is dedicated to my son, K. Richie Pound, who loves reading Ernest Hemingway novels, hunting, and fishing. He has always loved dogs. He has never been a fan of money.

PART ONE

Chapter One

For the love of money is a root of all kinds of evil.
I Timothy 5:10 (ESV)

During her lifetime Lula only knew that she had come from slaves, but her descendants later learned that only one of her grandparents had been a slave. Her grandfather had been the white master.

More than once, Lula had been quoted as saying, "If you is hoeing, or picking a row, or sweeping a yard, don't look back till you nearing the end, because if you keep looking back, you'll think you ain't getting nowhere, and you ain't never gonna get to the end. Keep your eyes straight ahead, and you'll see you is inching closer and closer to the finish. Then's the time you look back and see how far you is come."

It takes us most of our lives to know who we really are. We don't begin to see who we have become until we notice how the people around us have put their marks on our stories.

After Moe and Marty heard all the stories, they could make a little sense of their own lives. All that had happened to Moe during his life, shrouded in mystery, had created the chilly ostracism in which he lived. He had been born into a family of people already dead to him. Then he was shut off from people of lesser means on the outside. His estranged family had existed within self-imposed walls of frozen isolation. Was the root of the problem money or *lack* of it? Furthermore, was another major problem love or the *lack* of it? Had his doom been sealed by his family or by outsiders? And for Marty, he'd been searching for something all of his life and didn't know what—only that it was much bigger than anything he had ever had. Was it his quest for a father—or for the knowledge of a *heavenly Father?*

Money and time are intertwined in men's minds even for people who never have money and not enough time to make it. It was like that in Britton's Neck, a place of poor men. Some people said they thought there was a time they didn't have to work and sweat so hard for a living, but exactly when it was, they couldn't rightly remember. The goodhearted people of the godforsaken place in the triangle between the two rivers, the Big Pee Dee with its rusty waters, and the tea-colored Little Pee Dee, scrapped the earth for existence and prayed God would provide. Why had he put such a burden on them to till the soil to eke out their bread under the continuous rotation of glaring summer sun and winter wind? To make matters worse, they saw the Lackeys living off their old money. Even if they'd had hard times, the Lackeys were not of the same cut. The Lackeys were more equal to God, Britton's Neckers would say as they beat their chests and once in awhile their wives. For most of them, it was plain and simple: To some folks, money is given by God, and to others, it ain't. You should let it go at that and be thankful for what God did give you, which might be even better than money—like peace of mind. But for a few others, they could explain having money as God's favor, God deemed some more worthy than others and to those he gave lots of money, and people should work to gain God's favor, so they could get in on the riches too. But there was another group of people who believed God had nothing to do with money: Money had come from the devil, and if you wanted it, you'd have to shake hands with the devil himself to get it.

Moe Lackey, that is to say, Davis Moses Lackey, III, was now the only Lackey in Britton's Neck except for his mother, Violet. His sister Hazeline, who was ten years older than he, had run away, under nebulous conditions, when he was only six and had not been heard from since. He vaguely remembered the upheaval and mystery, the shushed whispering, the screaming and shouting behind closed doors, the crying wafting through the rafters of the mansion during the midnights of his early childhood and hearing the word *detectives* and conjuring up Dick Tracy in the funny papers. He had been too young to comprehend the significance of a few secret letters exchanged by his mother and her upstate relatives. The innuendos Britton's Neck folks made about his missing sister led him to believe she had been smart. Since she was smart, no one would hold his breath waiting for Hazeline Lackey to return to the two-rut rural Marion County farmland that she was born into and above.

Out of the Lackey's earshot, when old people talked in uncertainties that barely hint of the gospel truth, they always prefaced discussion of the Lackeys by noting how everyone else, "not me, mind you," questioned the credibility of the Lackeys. Where did they come from? Hadn't they come from the lowcountry of Georgetown where they went to worship and lay their dead? Hadn't the family lost a great-uncle in World War I, and didn't Moe's own father, Davis Moses

Lackey, Junior, try to serve the country?

That much was true. Davis Lackey had tried to enlist in the Second World War at the age of thirty-eight. If he had been accepted, he would have no doubt been among the nearly three percent of South Carolinian casualties of World War II. However, as badly as they needed men, he was turned down. Nevertheless, he died anyway before the age of forty either from grief over a lost daughter or his wife Violet's eccentricities afterwards. At any rate, after Davis Lackey's death, the world closed in around the two remaining Lackeys as if they were in a cocoon.

Later, as Moe grew, Violet became a wounded butterfly who couldn't flutter her wings without her son being somewhere near in the cage—the stately anachronistic mansion that sat in the shade at the end of the oak-lined driveway—the landmark used when anyone unfamiliar to Britton's Neck needed directions. Like some ill-practiced artist's rendition of Hera's dwelling, the mansion had a wide veranda with eight Corinthian heart pine columns—bars, impenetrable. The twin chimneys enclosed the wooden structure tightly on either side high above the tin roof. The once manicured grounds with all the intricate brick walkways meandering through camellias, azaleas, and dogwoods had become a haven for the primordial Yellow Jessamine that seemed to spring from every pore in the earth like a fanatical parasite with a mission to entangle and bury all living organisms on the mansion site.

The butterfly briefly emerged during her son's school days only to revert tighter into her cocoon when Moe went away to college and medical school. People knew that Hannah, her colored help of unknown age to herself as well as others, had at times taken up residence in the mansion to help care for her during some of the cocoon years. At long last, when Moe came home a full-fledged doctor, Violet appeared to have changed for the better.

It was unheard of that a doctor would practice in a small sandhill place like Britton's Neck, but when he hung his DR. M. LACKEY, MD shingle on the side of Highway 908 between Centenary and Conway, Britton's Neck suddenly became a Mecca of sorts. Marion and Conway businessmen pursed their lips and wrinkled their foreheads wondering why anyone with that much education would sign his own death certificate. Talk loomed that perhaps he didn't really need to practice medicine; he could live off old money for the rest of his life. Or maybe he just didn't have the stuff doctors were made of and couldn't open a practice in a competitive area. To townspeople twenty miles northwest in Marion, something was awry; no sane young man would start a career in Britton's Neck, South Carolina. But in spite of the skepticism, progress plowed ahead full throttle. Moe built a small office out on the highway to the side of the live oak trees lining the mansion's driveway. Not many buildings were near. Mt. Nebo Baptist Church was a mile to the north. Britton's Neck School and two-story teacherage, colored school, post office, Grange Hall, and construction site for the African Methodist Episcopal (AME) church were a quarter of a mile to the south. The only other public building was Williams' store, which was on the opposite side of the highway.

The Williams didn't know it at the time, but the day Moe opened his practice, their little business was on the eve of being revolutionized. Indeed, the little place on the map called Britton's Neck was at the epiphany of a new day. The very day that the first patient walked into Dr. Lackey's office, it was as if a freeway had been opened; a steady stream of pharmaceutical salesman appeared, streaming first into the new office and second into Williams' store.

James Vereen was all ears as Buck Bishop of Columbia raved what a killing somebody could make by opening a drugstore out here in the boonies. Vereen drank his Pepsi Cola and munched with each swig the Lance peanuts he had poured into the bottle. He listened quietly. As soon as James Vereen could introduce himself and his line of revolutionary medicines and leave a carton of this samples, he cancelled his plans to cross over into Florence County for his regular visits and made a bee line back across the Little Pee Dee toward Red Hill to his daddy's place.

All he needed was the financial backing. He had heard enough and knew that an opportunity like this only comes knocking once, but he better jump on it before someone else beat him to it. Old Mr. Vereen had land between Conway and Little River—lots of land that he hoped to pass on to grandchildren, lots of grandchildren, one day. Selling a few acres to turn into ready cash would still leave thousands of acres of prime timberland for his heirs. It would not be missed, and besides, his young son's ambition had always made him proud. It was a done deal.

Vereen drove across the Little Pee Dee to Britton's Neck for the third time in one day, and he drank another Pepsi Cola and ate another couple packs of Lance nabs with Tom Williams. Tom called his wife Shirley over to see how she would take to the idea. No, she would never sell the grocery store. Her daddy had run the store up until he died. Right away, James Vereen got the picture—it was really Williams' wife's business, but how do you deal with a woman? After about an hour of fast talking and picture painting, Tom and Shirley Williams promised they could think about it and let him know before the week was out if they would sell the store or maybe a half acre adjoining their property to put a little business which would not compete with theirs. They promised that they would not discuss this interest with outsiders.

It is surprising how dreams are spawned with the mention of money. Shirley Williams dreamed dreams during the night that before today had been as foreign as Paris, France. Within no time, Vereen's Drug Store was stocking up, and Shirley Williams was buying new shoes with matching pocketbooks at B.C. Moores & Sons in Marion and driving by the Ford place to see what this year's new automobiles looked like. Vereen had talked to two of his Conway buddies who were pharmacists about a job rotation plan at his new Britton's Neck drug store. They knew James Vereen enough to know he must be onto something big. They were interested and thought they could finagle a way to keep their regular jobs by cutting back days with no problems in sight.

Like Shirley Williams, the tobacco farmers and their wives had not realized they had been waiting their whole lives for just such a momentous event. Now, people from all the little patches of farmland within a fifteen-mile radius—Britton's Neck, Woodberry, Gresham, Fellowship, Johnsonville, and Centenary—didn't have to bum a ride or load up the automobile to drive to Marion, Mullins, or Conway to see a doctor if one of the youngins was bent over double for a few weeks or if they had been spitting up blood. They would have their own doctor, and they would have their own drugstore.

All at once, the world looked healthier than it had ever looked. It was an omen for sure. Seeing the doctor became the conversation of fashionable practice. Getting a prescription was good; having to get two filled was even weightier in any circle besides talking about how much each little pill cost. Dreams grew bigger and bigger. The doctor's office and Vereen's Drug Store would one day be a clinic. The clinic would one day be a hospital. People could have surgery in a hospital. Mothers began to tell their little towheaded boys that they could grow up to become a doctor like Dr. Lackey and their girls that they could grow up to be nurses. Nothing better could be imagined for Britton's Neck. How amazing were the wondrous things of the Lord! As the vicinity glowed with the promise of better health, no one could have diagnosed the sickness that would silently creep into the sandhills.

Chapter Two

He that is of the opinion money will do everything
may well be suspected of doing everything for money.
Ben Franklin

Every year at Britton's Neck School, four skinny, field-tanned high school boys were selected to drive the school buses for a whopping $15 a month. All others rode the bus. That is, except for Martin Price, who rode to school with his mother, one of the two cafeteria workers, and Moe Lackey, who, during the time he was a junior and senior of Britton's Neck School, drove the short distance to school from the mansion in his practically new 1946 maroon Oldsmobile sedan and parked it beside the teachers' cars—drabber and older, mostly V8 Fords. Teachers, who carpooled to the country school from Marion or Mullins, often jabbed each other and joked about the red Olds, the rose among the thorns, but somehow it wasn't really funny after their cramped twenty-mile ride.

To the left of the schoolhouse was the teachers' parking area consisting of about twenty feet of green grass most of the school year and sandy clay the rest of the time. The strip of lawn separated the school from about fifty acres of Mr. Hoyt Richardson's cornfields. If you were driving around the school, you'd pass the teachers' cars and the clump of pine trees where the little children rushed during recess to play sling the biscuit or to build pine straw forts. Then after passing the pine trees, you'd see the lunchroom, its bright-whiteness like a heavenly portal beyond the pines and in the foreground of the deep woods. The lunchroom, long and narrow, had a low roofline, a few windows on each side, and a single door on the side where children lined up to enter the lunchroom as if they were entering the pearly gates. The two lunchroom workers parked at the edge of the woods and came in through the back door.

If you continued driving around the school, like the buses did, rounding the back curve, you'd see on the left about fifty yards or so the auto mechanics shop. Occasionally, a school bus would be hoisted up on half its wheels to be worked on by the auto mechanics teacher and class and sometimes the school district maintenance men. Two classes were held in the mechanics shop, auto mechanics and agriculture. Continuing driving around the school, the only other thing you'd see was a clay field farther on around to the left where the bigger students organized and played baseball during recess.

It was an understatement to say that Violet Lackey and her son had few friends, but during a brief interlude of Moe's high school years before his 1950 graduation and leaving for the University of South Carolina, she, with the assistance of Polly, one of the school lunchroom workers, and Hannah hosted several teas for new teachers, school administrators, and members of the school board. Few people in Britton's Neck had attempted to scale the impervious wall of the mansion. Mrs. Violet, the wounded butterfly, and Moe, the reclusive boy, were observed from a distance except for Moe's only friend, Marty Price, Polly's son, who understood several things about Moe Lackey, most of all his maroon 1946 Oldsmobile.

Chapter Three

There is no class so pitiably wretched as that which possesses money and nothing else.

Andrew Carnegie

Except for a short period of time, Martin Price, like Moe, had lived alone with his mother. In 1950, he and Moe turned off Highway 908 onto Highway 378 in Moe's '46 Olds and headed straight for the South Carolina state capital of Columbia where Marty was going to join the Army and Moe to enroll in the University of South Carolina. One of them said, "See ya later, alligator," and the other said, "After while, crocodile" when Moe dropped Marty off at the gates of Fort Jackson. It would have looked to a passerby as a casual exchange, but it was, in fact, tumultuous for each of the two boys.

A couple of years earlier, during his tenth grade year, Marty had started erecting a concrete block shed beside his mother's house where he worked on cars. After awhile, he added a crude bathroom. Then he partitioned off a section for a bed and radio. Gradually this had become his own house, a declaration of independence from his mother, Polly Price, whose small wood frame house could be seen from the highway. Marty's small abode was partially hidden by the low spreading limbs of an ancient live oak tree. Moe Lackey's '46

Olds was often parked beneath the overhanging oak limbs. After graduation from the University, Moe replaced the Olds with a 1953 Mercury Monterey, and if Moe Lackey was in Britton's Neck during his medical school days, most likely the red Monterey could be seen beneath the sagging branches of the venerable oak. Often, a strand of the tree's Spanish moss flew in the wind, a banner, on the Monterey's aerial on his return to school. Talk was that Martin Price, even with his limp and sour disposition, made a couple trips to Charleston during Moe's medical school days, but somehow managed to get in scraps with sailors from the naval base every time he was there. He vowed each time that Charleston would never lay eyes on old Marty Price again.

Finally, after Charleston and a residency in Savannah, Moe came home and began doctoring in 1957. Violet opened the cage again, but the teas for the teachers were a thing of the past. She was now her son's receptionist. The butterfly, as nurse-receptionist, flitted around her son and his patients. She made files for each patient, recording and updating information meticulously. Since there were fewer than a dozen telephones in Britton's Neck, and all of them party lines, Violet insisted to Blanche at the telephone company that they put a private line to the doctor's office. She personally visited Mr. Samuel Goldstein, who ran the most expensive furniture store in Marion, with measurements she had taken herself for sofas and chairs. Within two weeks, Mr. Goldstein, who had heard about the new country doctor, delivered the waiting room furniture himself—four long pink and grey vinyl sofas with modern metal legs, eight matching chairs, and two magazine tables. The furniture was divided equally between the white and colored waiting rooms. Violet, who had been a Book of the Month member for years, chose reading materials she felt suitable for the patients: *The Progressive Farmer*, *The Marion Star*, and *McCalls*.

Even before her daughter had disappeared years earlier, Violet had been concealed from view and open only to the imagination. Britton's Neck people who had never been privileged to know Violet Lackey could now see a part of the mosaic of the mansion. With the doctor's doors opened, farm folks couldn't help but stare at the lily-white woman with the soft arms and widening hips. They observed the snowy edging around the round face and the lines beginning to map the eyes and mouth and forehead. They wondered why she had been so mysteriously appealing—she looked not as old as they had presumed but as common as they, except for her eyes. People said they had never seen eyes so blue, like two sparkling cutouts of the sky. Still, maybe there was an unidentifiable element in her fiber that marked her as different from them, the ordinary people. After all, she was old rich, and *those eyes*.

It was for certain she had more stamina at fifty-two than they had reckoned. Mrs. Violet spent entire days in the doctor's office, registering patients and calling them back to the examination rooms. Single-handedly, she worked along with her son until the day was done at 4:45. Then she turned the CLOSED sign around and locked the doors first on the colored side and then on the white side. Only if someone hammered continuously, did she open the doors after 4:45 P.M. Usually, in that case, there was a baby to be born, or there had been a farm accident like the time the horse reared back and kicked Rufus, knocking him minus several teeth and half his senses. Folks got used to Rufus without all of his teeth, but they never adjusted to the senseless Rufus. They had to remind each other with every mention of his name why he acted as he did.

The doctor's mother, protective of her son, was intuitive about emergencies and real sicknesses and more than intuitive when young girls and wives of the county made appointments and came in dressed in Sunday clothes and daubed with Evening in Paris cologne. Even though his taciturn behavior never wavered, Dr. Lackey might have been relieved that Nurse Lackey was present. Who can tell what goes on the minds of the privileged? And who can tell what goes on in the minds of poor young white girls and their mothers who have never been more than twenty miles from Britton's Neck? Who can tell whose thoughts are like Rufus'— mangled and twisted?

Chapter Four

If women didn't exist, all the money
in the world would have no meaning.
Aristotle Onassis

Martin Price had returned from Korea in 1953 with his body jerking spasmodically and supporting his weak leg with a cane. His friend, Moe, had four more years of medical school, so no one thought a thing about his excessive concern for Marty—Moe was a friend who was learning to be a doctor. No one suspected their friendship could be anything other than platonic, except maybe morons like Rufus.

Martin Price's return to Britton's Neck signaled the beginning of a dark epoch. Martin's deranged physical appearance was not incomparable to his demeanor. Always a loner except for his relationship with Moe Lackey, he was never cheerful or outgoing, but now he was rendered incapable of gaiety in any form. He was surly, showing contempt for everything and everyone who did not get out of his path. His demented mood most poignantly affected his mother whose sole purpose his entire life had been to right her wrong and see that he was happier than she had ever been herself.

Her thirty-seven year old body had gradually begun to fight on the enemy's side of her emotional battle. Her sister

Blanche tried to coax Polly to see a doctor. "You can afford it," her sister said. "You've never in your life paid one bit of attention to yourself. I tell you, Polly, you don't look good. You don't act right. Something is eating you away inside. You need to see the doctor."

Pauline Price had always been nondescript, but her life had conformed her to be docile, patient, and kind. She stared ahead at vacant years, and when she turned her head, she only saw a vacant past, except for a few weeks of happiness with a man she should never have looked at, let alone walked to the river to meet on a moonlit night. Maybe when she was a teenager, if she'd been a little prettier like her sister, and maybe if her hair had not been so curly and fiery red, and maybe if she had been less big-boned and more feminine, then maybe some decent man would have looked at her. But maybe God had the plan already set, and his plan was that she would be left out of ever having a husband. She'd heard that God had a match somewhere for everyone. Maybe folks who came up with that saying were mistaken. Maybe he never intended for every person on the face of the planet to have a mate. Weren't there nuns and priests and friars and monks who vowed celibacy? If God meant for everyone to have a soul mate, maybe she had messed up God's plan for her life when she walked to the river.

On the other hand, maybe God had not thought about what the Great Depression would do to young men—making them want to join the Army to get a warm meal three times a day even if there was war talk that England and France were getting ready to fight Germany—fight the Crouts to put the hated Hitler machine out of commission and stop German aggression. These sweet young men didn't know—they had no idea at the time—that the world was on the verge of hell, and that a little less than seven million Jews plus a goodly number of homosexuals and mentally challenged human beings in Europe would be mercilessly killed. Not only that, but all the potential husbands of all the poor ugly Pollys in the United States would bleed their good American blood away on foreign dirt in an effort to save these people they had never seen or heard of and would never see, and probably wouldn't have anything to do with if they did. They—those sweet, innocent, lovely, young men—would be making unmarried girls like Polly grow old cursed and alone.

Just when Polly's sixteen-year-old body was aching for attention, the county sheriff's office brought the chain gang to work the country roads. It would be twenty years before Britton's Neck highways would have a tar top. Working the road meant digging ditches for water to drain off, filling in major holes with clay, and removing overhanging tree limbs from roadside trees that were likely to fall on the roadways. And working the roads meant jailbirds could get fresh air and exercise, and the county could get a return on the debt of keeping them out of society's way.

The officer in charge of the manacled men with the shovels and pick axes was Alvin Dozier. He drove the truck with the chained men in the back from Marion to Britton's Neck every morning. Every day, it moved closer and closer to Winston Price's farm. Before leaving for his fields, Winston warned his wife and daughters to lock up in the house and "don't darsn't open a door nor a window, no matter what." But when the chain gang had gotten within earshot, and as soon as the mailman, Mr. Johnston Coleman, approached the mailbox, young Pauline burst from the front door and jumped down the steps as if she had been catapulted from a cannon at a circus, and then slowly and deliberately she sashayed down to the mailbox, taking her time opening and closing the mailbox door.

Mr. Johnston Coleman, a father himself and a member of the school board, spat out the words in as kindly a reprimand as possible, "Miss Polly, you better be careful coming out here with those prisoners so close to yall's house. Go on inside now and help your mama with the canning I 'spect she's doing."

"Mr. Johnston, you sound just like my daddy. Those men are chained. I really don't see why they have to be chained like that. They ain't gonna try to escape. Where in the world would they escape to anyway? That officer would shoot their head off, I expect." She looked toward the uniformed officer with the rifle down by his leg. He had his hat off and was mopping his forehead. "I'd like to take them some water to drink. It's so hot and dusty. And the way they're digging and stuff."

"Pauline Price, you git in that house and stay away from those convicts, you hear me!" He meant to say a word to Winston the next time he saw him. He thought about how hot it would be in a few hours, and, being the only mailman for all the area of Britton's Neck and Gresham, he knew he had a lot of route left to drive. He changed gears, and his truck chugged along.

Polly pretended to walk back toward the house, and then pretended to see a flower on the side of the road that she wanted to salvage before the prisoners' tools reached it. Six of the seven convicts had quit work and were leaning on their shovels making low remarks to each other, all except the one black man who appeared to work steadily without so much as lifting his head. The officer snapped sharply for the men to get back to work, and simultaneously lifted his rifle. He then walked toward the place where Polly stooped to pluck the maypop blossom, a milky white and lavender flower on a vine with tentacles. It would wilt in five minutes, and she knew it. Still she held it as if it were the most treasured mystery she had ever seen. She could hear the officer's shoes hit a clod of dirt, and she turned just as he was within three feet of her.

"Ma'am, you sure are brave for such a pretty girl. Most folks see the gang coming and lock up tigher'er a drum."

"I ain't *most folks*." She lifted her eyes to see that he was not too old, and he was looking at her face, and a sly smile was spreading across his face. He had dark eyes. He was not exactly handsome, but, individually, all his features looked good. His smile revealed wide teeth. From her window, she had noticed that he usually had a cigarette in his mouth, but he didn't now. His nose was thin and came to a point. He was "as tanned as a berry" as her ma would say. And his hair was thick and black. He took off his hat and ran his fingers backward through his hair.

"How do you do, ma'am? I'm Officer Alvin Dozier with the Marion County Sheriff's Department and what might your pretty little name be?"

She had never been introduced to anyone in her whole life, and now she wanted to appear that she knew how to be proper.

"I'm Pauline Price, sir, and pleased to make your acquaintance."

"Sir? You don't haf' to call me *sir*. I don't reckon I'm much older than you. How old are you anyway? You married?"

To this absurd question, which had caught her off guard, she laughed freely. Then she turned serious. "I wish. I wish I *was married* and far away from *this* place and this here county where nothing ever happens. If I was a boy, I'd *sign up* and go in the Army.

"You sure have an exciting job. Do they ever try to break out? Did you ever have to shoot one of 'em?"

"Sure. You see, they're dangerous men. There's one thought in every single one of 'em's head—when can I make my move?"

Her eyes widened and then narrowed as she glanced around him and saw all of them. Even the black man, now had stopped his work and was leaning on his rake like the others, leaning on their shovels or hoes looking at Dozier's back. "Yeah, they sure do look mean. What all did they do to get locked up?"

"Murder. Rob banks. Remember over in Florence County a couple years ago? That boy and girl got their heads cut off and throwed in a well?"

She gasped, and he laughed. "Well, that fellow ain't on this gang. They still don't know where he is. Florence County is bad about never catching their man, but it's different in Marion County. You ain't got nothing to worry about. Nothing."

Polly almost didn't hear the screen door open. But she heard her ma's voice trying to yell in a constrained manner. "Polly, Polly, come here, child."

"Your ma's calling. It was nice meeting you, Miss Polly Prince."

"Price! My name is Miss Polly *Price*."

"'Cuse me. Thank you for setting me straight. I won't make that mistake again, Miss Pre—ice."

Chapter Five

What good is money if it can't inspire
terror in your fellow man?
Monty Burns

Polly's mother had seen the uniformed man conversing with her older daughter and could not resist a sense of pride that an important man would take notice of her girl. She also felt a sense of sympathy for her daughter who longed for companionship. Heaven knows, the days were long enough as it was, and summer getting riper and riper, and though the nights were getting shorter and shorter, the evenings were getting longer and longer. Saturday nights when the family gathered around the radio to listen to the Grand Ole Opry, she would notice the abject loneliness on the older girl's face. Already sixteen, and she had never held a personal conversation with anyone of the opposite sex.

Polly walked pass her mother as if her ma were a stranger. She walked back to the back porch pump and automatically poured the water down the pump head to prime it. Then she yanked the handle up and slammed it down time and time again until the pressure built, and she knew the water was caught. Water gushed forth from the iron spout. She looked off through the screened porch and continued to pump with her right hand, letting the water flow over her left hand into the enamel sink until she felt it was cool, and there was no grit in it. She quickly slapped both hands full of water over her face, letting it roll down her neck, her shoulders, and her chest.

"What are you doing? You're getting your dress all wet!" Her sister Blanche yelled. Blanche, two years younger than Polly, was not exactly what people would call beautiful, but people could not resist commenting when they saw her that she was the pretty one. Blanche's hair was a glorious auburn and wavy, naturally calm and tame, whereas, Polly's hair was frizzy as if all the wildness in the Price DNA had been spent on Polly. Blanche was the only person in the world who never noticed that Polly was one notch up from being downright ugly. And it was Blanche who was ever attempting to hone Polly's mannerisms, coaxing her in some aspects of femininity.

"Polly," Blanche reprimanded, "Daddy's gonna whip you when he gits home for being out there at that road. Is your brain dried up from too much sun?"

"He said, 'What's your pretty little name, Miss?'"

"Did he? What'd you say?"

"He said, 'Ain't you scared of the chain gang? Most folks are.' Then I said, 'I ain't most folks.'"

"My! Now didn't you sound mighty biggity," said Nadine Price through the kitchen screen door. She spat a mouthful of snuff and saliva out into the yard as she shoved aside the screened door.

"Ma, the sheriff said they ain't dangerous."

"Then why is they on the gang, young lady?"

"They were drunk or something like that. You think they'd

put dangerous people out where decent folks live?"

"I still can't see why they don't ship jailbirds oversees to fight and let decent boys stay at home right where they belong."

"Me either, Ma."

Nadine turned and went inside to the wood stove to tend the fresh butterbeans she was cooking and the canning she was in process of doing. She had learned to cook in summer with the fire low in the burner, not roaring so that the kitchen got muggy hot. Usually she cooked the dinner in the morning, but today she had picked two bushels of the blue-speckled butterbeans at first light before the truck with the chain gang occupants arrived. She and her girls had shelled one bushel already, and by this time tomorrow, she would have canned these and twenty quarts of tomatoes to feed the family during the short winter days that would surely come.

The fatback grease shimmered on top of the beans. A hoe cake and the beans and a glass of clabber would set Winston in a good mood for sure, she hoped.

Chapter Six

I made a conscious decision to earn enough to be able to choose my husband rather than not have a career and marry someone who would have to earn enough for us both to live on.

Sarah Beeny

Nine months and two weeks later, when Polly's husky body revolted and rebelled against giving birth, it was Blanche who scurried around the room over the low bed, heating water and sterilizing the knife. The black midwife finally pulled out the red mummy that was attached to the purplish-blue cord and slapped its back until it screamed. Then the white-palmed hands deftly cleaned up the baby and next the mother. Blanche continued to dance about, thinking Polly would never regain life. Polly's motionless body, mind, and spirit indicated all of her life had been drawn out in the form of an eight-pound baby leaving only a drenched, pale shell. When she failed to respond, the black woman looked at Blanche.

"Go git ya mamma," she said to Blanche. "And don't ya waste no time gitting back."

Polly had made Blanche swear on the family Bible that neither her father nor mother would be there when the time came. Since her daddy had half killed her while her mother had stood by not raising a hand to stop him, she mentally and emotionally had cut ties to both of them. She had signed a disclaimer with irrevocable terms in her heart and mind.

Winston and Nadine Price had put their daughter in the empty sharecropper's shack near their house and fabricated a loosely threaded tale about a secret marriage to a soldier. No one believed the story but Winston and Nadine Price, and after months of telling it, the shack symbolized the truth of the lie.

Blanche was mystified to see her mother already up in the middle of the night as if she had some prophetic vision that tonight would be the night. Nadine was sitting at the table over a cup of strong black coffee, freshly made. The lantern light made a contrasting circle about her haggard face and the open Bible she had before her.

"Ma! You gotta come! The baby's come! Things ain't right! Polly—she ain't moving. Her eyes are open but she looks—"

Nadine clenched her teeth, clasped her hands together under the bowed head and seemed to demand something of God. Then she stood and finished off the cup and led Blanche back to the shack.

In the dim lantern light, Nadine easily saw the three figures—Lula, tiny, wrinkled and black, holding the tiny, wrinkled and red bundle, and on the cot the drowned-looking Pauline. Life even appeared to have departed from the usual overly vivacious red hair. Nadine bent over the body, grabbed both shoulders and spoke slowly and low, "Pauline Price, you better hear me, girl. Get a holt of yourself right now! Get a holt of yourself! You just had a youngin that you gotta live and raise! Listen to me! Now sit up!"

Polly turned toward the woman, "Ma? What is it?"

Nadine looked up at Lula.

"He a boy," Lula said hoarsely.

Nadine reached for the infant and put the boy at Polly's bosom. He automatically sucked. "Ain't no milk now, little fella, but hit'll come. Right now, it's like water; but the milk'll come later."

Polly looked down then at the slick black head, and her arms and hands moved to support the tiny creature. For the next eighteen years and beyond, in fact, the rest of her life, Polly's only focus in life was to do just that.

Chapter Seven

The chief value of money lies in the fact that one lives in a world in which it is overestimated.

H. L. Mencken

The circle had nearly made itself back to its beginning. Blanche had married one of the first men to survive Pearl Harbor and return to Britton's Neck. Harold Fitzgibbons was from one the first families to come to Britton's Neck along with the Brittons themselves—Daniel, Francis, Joseph, Moses, Philip, and Timothy. According to legend, Colonel Lucius Fitzgibbons had led a guerrilla band in fighting the Tories along with Francis Marion, the Swamp Fox, up and down the swamps from Woodberry to Georgetown. The trouble with history books was that there was never a mention of Colonel Fitzgibbons. Francis Marion was easier to remember, and the Swamp Fox conjured up more to the imagination. The Fitzgibbons family had felt jilted for nearly two hundred years and blamed their every shortcoming on historians.

And Harold was not to be blamed for coming back from overseas a drunkard. He had seen too many body parts fly from their original location. He had heard too many shells pop too close to his eardrums. It took more and more alcohol to help him fall into temporary memory lapse. To Blanche, Harold's drinking did not matter at first. To Walter and Nadine, it never mattered at all. He was a man who was their daughter's husband. He would be a father to any children Blanche would have. Both of them went to their graves thinking that Blanche might yet produce a grandchild of whom they could boast.

But they let their childbearing years pass them by. Marty was nine years old when Blanche and Harold got married, and he was as close to being theirs as any child could have been. Later when Martin returned from Korea suffering from the effects of jellied gasoline, called napalm, burned into his flesh, Harold never criticized Marty's anger at the world. In fact, Marty's limp served to bring the two closer together like natural father and son. Harold could overlook and forgive any act of Marty's. Marty dignified Harold's own Pearl Harbor stories, even though Marty never once mentioned a single battle he himself had endured.

In spite of Marty's heftiness at birth, when he had entered first grade, he found all the other children his age taller and bigger, even the girls. He was to be the runt of the class for the remainder of his school years—the first in line for recess or lunch. The class line was the only thing in which Marty was first; however, at a later, more researched and informed time in American education, Marty might have been referred by a classroom teacher to undergo psychological analysis and then diagnosed as having an attention deficient disorder or dyslexia or some other various label for not being able to take pen and paper tests with eighty-percent proficiency. Marty could not sit still in one of the desks in one of the rows in a warm classroom with a wall of windows where he could see the sun shining outside on all that green grass and blue sky.

From his desk at the back of the room, he could barely see the cars and trucks pass on Highway 908, but he could certainly hear them, and he began to fine tune the sounds of the motors. He began to know before the vehicle passed what kind of automobile it was.

Yes, had Marty lived forty or fifty years later, he would have been stigmatized as a non-learner or resource student. But this was before that time in America when all students and all schools were ranked in order of achievements on pen and paper tests, and before South Carolina was ranked on the bottom of the educational scale, and students like Marty on the bottom of the bottom. So Marty Price and all the other Marty Prices like him were simply left in the classroom and to their own imaginations year after year.

And their imaginations were not idle, at least Marty's wasn't—his worked overtime. Since his mother worked in the lunchroom, the teachers would often appease his stubbornness by telling him that if he felt sick, he had permission to go to his mother. Then he would lie around on the lunchroom pantry floor, but more often than not, he would wander next door to the mechanics shop. While the teachers could not teach the unwilling Marty algebra and English grammar, he was learning something useful just the same. By the time he graduated from high school, he was able to teach the maintenance men how to fix bus motors as well as any other motor they brought into the shop. That knowledge would benefit him when he found himself on the other side of the globe in the constant rumble of military tanks.

On the other end of the spectrum of academia was Moe, but he was just as isolated as Marty. By eighth grade, the two had discovered each other, and they were inseparable. Moe found a way to help Marty pass his classes, and Marty tinkered with the Oldsmobile and made Moe feel he was not entirely alone in the world. Another solidifying force was the fact that Polly was proficient in baking petit fours and making pineapple cream cheese sandwiches and was the hands for Violet's culinary ideas during Violet's gregarious years. Polly and Marty were at the mansion more than anyone else other than Hannah. The bond between the two boys became sealed even though life would send them out in separate directions in the future. Moe would be learning how to save life by playing with cadavers while Marty would be learning about death by seeing boys his age become cadavers.

It appeared that the Korean War was begun for the sole purpose of justifying the life of Martin Price. He heard the news of North Korea's attack on South Korea the last of June while still dazed over being out of school. Ironically, though he hated school, school had been his life, his real home for the past twelve years. Being graduated now from school had produced an additional sense of lostness. He had no reason to belong there or anywhere else for that matter. The radio broadcasts about the conflict in Korea began to fill a void at precisely the time everything else seemed to be fizzling out.

His grandmother's brother-in-law ran a store in Little River near Myrtle Beach. A few times during his life they had visited, and Polly had allowed him to stay a few days to help out during the summer when they had a higher than usual volume of customers from the North. Only in the summer did people other than locals come into the store to chat, checking on weather conditions for fishing. Each summer seemed to bring more and more traffic from northerners who asked lots of questions about property on the coast, and each year another two or three stilt houses went up on the beach. Consequently, local farmers turned carpenters were getting jobs building vacation houses which allowed them better means to feed their houseful of barefooted children.

After 1950 graduation, Marty, still disconnected and uncertain, thought maybe he would leave the Neck and make a new life for himself in Little River. Uncle Louis was getting up in age. Aunt Thelma was not as much help in the store anymore since her rheumatoid arthritis had set in nearly crippling her. Since they had no children, the idea arose that he might take over the little gas station one day when his Uncle Louis could no longer keep it up. More than anything, Marty loved to pump gas for the customers who drove their automobiles up under the Shell sign and the twin gas pumps.

He could hear the cars before they ever stopped and would run through the screen door letting it flap with a bang. He wouldn't bother offering a word or nod in the way of greeting before he'd begin turning the crank for the gas. Then he would take the old rags and wash the windshield while evaluating every part of the car and the maintenance it had or had not had in the past. Often he would ask questions like, "How many miles ya got on 'er?" "When did you put in oil last?" "How fast does she go?" "Do you mind if I just look at her motor?"

Local people were patient, even appreciative, as Marty inspected every mechanism under the hood and made adjustments. But the non-locals would mumble something about being in a hurry, thinking some curious hick kid couldn't possibly know whether it was a six or eight cylinder. Those who allowed Marty to plunder around under the hood often discovered that their car ran smoother and used less gas, and later when they returned, they'd ask Louis, "Where is that little fellow you had working for you a while back? I'd like to ask him something."

On her good days, Aunt Thelma worked in her patch of a garden growing a few hills of corn, okra, butterbeans, peas, squash, and tomatoes. Their little wood frame house sat in back of the store surrounded by a leaning rusty fence that kept in her half dozen or so chickens. If Marty was around, she treated him like a child, constantly wanting him to "run check on your Uncle Louis." "Bring me back a hunk of cheese." "Help me pick this little row of butterbeans before dark." "Would you take a minute to collect the day's eggs?" "Lean the porch chairs against the house before we go inside." "Run bring me the mail." The thought of helping to run the store was enticing and having evenings to drive down to the ocean alone was tantalizing, but after several weeks of Aunt Thelma's constant menial chores, Marty jumped at the chance of doing carpenter work with one of the Loris builders who stopped in to fill his tank with $2.00 worth of gasoline.

Marty had knowledge of motors and engines. The construction he'd done on his own little shed was with cement blocks. He had little knowledge of two-by-fours and six-penny nails. Once again, as he heard the burly men yelling constantly, "Marty, over here," he had a vague discontent with being the tote boy. The late July sun was already radiating the temperature upward in the nineties. August would be hotter still. On the strand there was no shady oak tree to mute the rays. *Hey*, Marty thought, *this is just one way to make a living.* Then he looked at the men with their powerful but stained hands. He did not mind stained hands—motor oil and car grease had left permanent stains under his fingernails. These men had strong arms and backs, but their faces were etched with lines beyond their years from working in the hard elements, lines deeper than the inlets from the Atlantic.

They crammed into the black pickup trucks, three or four to a pickup, with their black lunchboxes and drove the good part of an hour before the sun was up to begin hammering and sawing to build someone else a better house than they themselves would ever own. They withstood the sun and sawdust as long as they could and then piled their limp manhood back into the pickups to drive home in a cloud of Camel cigarette smoke. Back to Loris and to the little farms where they would feed up the mules, cows, hogs, and give instructions for their boys to do this, or that, or the other, the next day.

Under the blazing Horry County sun, Martin Price gazed at the horizon of the steel gray Atlantic Ocean. He remembered the war stories Uncle Harold had told as he had slipped slowly and surely into a drunken coma at the tobacco shed. Uncle Harold would pick up a discarded Coca Cola bottle and hurl it though the air at some imperceptible "son-of-a bitch Crout." Marty sensed Uncle Harold no longer had a European face attached to the curse, but to fate, itself, a force which decreed him to be a non-existent nobody in history's scheme of heroes and hobos. He had been one who gave his manhood to fight another man's battle and come away nameless. Marty, out of duty for all the Harold Fitzgibbons, or out of hate of all the heroes, began to realize he must go and add himself to the number of the nameless. He must pick up the mantel Harold had handed him sometime during the past eighteen years. His blood boiled as he thought of the bullies in Korea running over women, children, and old men.

His only friend, Moe Lackey, would be going to Columbia at the University of South Carolina—his future had long been settled—Moe would be a doctor—Mrs. Violet and Moe had always known that. Marty realized—his own fate was just as settled—but in the opposite direction.

Resolutely, Marty was handing up the lumber for the beach house being built for Mr. Renzulli from somewhere in the state of New Jersey. In fact, Mr. Renzulli himself had shown up with a fat Cuban cigar in his mouth. Every phrase he uttered was flanked with profanity and curses. He had called the Loris contractor down from the second floor where he was putting up interior walls.

"Why the hell, can't you get these goddamn Southern cotton pickers to work any faster? Jez Christ, I told you I wanted this goddamn house finished before the summer is over. I want to bring my family down to see the land that God forgot, so's they can get some sun."

Marty noticed the foreman's jaw twitching, swallowing the words he wanted to say—but wouldn't—and chewing over the words he'd been taught by God to use. When he spoke, it would be slow, deliberate, honest and humble. "Mr. Renzulli, sir, I told you when we took this job, it wouldn't be finished till end of August if'n you want it done good. My boys don't work sloppy, and I ain't figuring you want a haf-built house sitting here for a herri-cane to blow over."

"Ya. Ya," Mr. Renzulli growled, sucking on the cigar. "I got money tied up in this, and with this Korean thing, you never know what the market'll do." He went on as if he were talking to himself. "Just git a move on with it!"

Marty had been walking by to get more lumber to hoist up to the area where the hammering all but drowned out the low, peaceful sound of the ocean's waves. Mr. Renzulli turned just as Marty walked by and seemed unable to resist commenting on the scrawny half-size man.

"And what in Christ name! This goddamn kid. Doing absolutely nothing."

The man from Loris, himself a deacon in the Loris Free Will Baptist Church, albeit there were only forty members, was composing his words but didn't have time to speak. Marty did not chew his words. He stopped directly in front of the rotund New Jersey businessman.

"I ain't a goddamn kid. And I ain't doing 'absolutely nothing.' I'll show you what I can do."

The men on the roof and on the second floor stopped hammering and looked down at the pint-sized Britton's Neck nephew of Mr. Louis who ran the store in Little River where they gassed up once a week. Marty picked up three or four eight-foot pieces of pine lumber and walked back to within a few feet of Mr. Renzulli. Marty swung the lumber forcefully, hitting Mr. Renzulli midway his torso, sending the Cuban cigar catapulting to the sand and him bending double, gasping for breath. Marty had been very careful not to let the lumber strike the Loris deacon who was too much of a Christian not to turn the other cheek. He dropped the pine lumber between the two men.

Marty looked at the man who had given him his first official job. “I just ain’t cut out for this kinda work, sir. What you owe me, send to my Uncle Louis Cook. I’ll thumb a ride home.” Marty walked off, already feeling like a soldier.

Chapter Eight

Make money your god and it will
plague you like the devil.
Henry Fielding

During the ride through Fort Jackson with the busload of recruits, Marty was reflecting on the goodbye. He had just said, "Adieus. See you later, alligator," to which Moe had chimed, "After while, crocodile." Moe had dropped him off at the Fort Jackson gates, and Marty sensed he was still sitting at the entrance leaning against the gleaming fender of his '46 Oldsmobile, which Marty had lovingly patted and started to lean down to kiss before walking through the gates. These two knew more about each other than anything or anyone else in the world.

Both of these would-be men were deep in self-reflection and wondering. How much would the other change? Would this parting goodbyes mark a change in their relationship? Marty's thoughts revolved like the spin of a car motor. When he returned from oversees, would everything be different as if the past had been a movie that played at the theater for a month or so and then was gone? Would Moe be married or involved with someone? Would he ever feel equal to Moe again? After all, Moe was from another element. He was always in control. Moe was going to be a doctor. While he, himself, was probably going to forget the last shred of knowledge he had struggled all his life to learn in school, Moe, on the other hand, was going to use his vast knowledge as a diving board to gain even more, and then more, knowledge. It seemed unlikely that Moe could become any smarter. What would they ever have to talk about again?

Awkwardly, they had tried to say their goodbyes back in the Neck, and at the Fort Jackson entrance they tried to look casual as if they hardly knew each other, as if Moe had simply picked up a hitchhiker. Moe waited to be sure Marty went through the gate after talking a minute to the guard. On the outskirts of Columbia, he deliberately turned down a side street to lose himself to his thoughts. He knew he could find his way again to Blossom Street and then the USC campus and administration office.

During all the years growing up, Moe had felt encased by heavy dark damask draperies blocking out the sunlight. Solemn older people were the only relatives he and his mother ever visited. His mother, never cheerful, always sad, lonely, somber, existed only with the aid of Hannah and the other black people who did the occasional yard work. Hannah, more acquainted with his mother than anyone, came and went doing chores silently and cheerlessly.

He'd always thought that joy died with the loss of his sister and death of his father, but did it? Had there ever been joy and happiness in that mansion? He could not remember ever losing himself to laughter even as a child. He could not remember his father. He could not remember any experience that involved his sister. Periodically, he had looked at her school photo in the frame on the old mahogany spindle organ until it was the photo he saw in his mind, not her. Whenever he thought of her, she was frozen in time, looking serious with only that photograph smile. Maybe she had never smiled either. Maybe that is why she ran away—to search for somewhere bright where the sun could shine on her face, where she could finally smile. He never smiled in the mansion either. He was never expected to.

Now, in Columbia the prospect of being away from the mansion was ambivalent—exhilarating but terrifying. It would be different if Marty could be here with him to explore this new freedom. Marty had always been the only brightness to his dull life. He could talk Marty into doing anything up to a point: Marty ruled Marty.

In his young life, any escapes from the moldy atmosphere of the mansion had been through Martin. Martin had no adults who pressed and ironed his clothes, even his bed linens, his emotions, and his activities. Martin had always been free—his own man, doing what he thought he wanted to do. Moe sometimes confused his identity with Marty's, but sooner or later he had to reckon with the fact that Martin went back around the bay where no one controlled the elements. Didn't everyone know that Giles Bay was the area of the Little Pee Dee River that no man could control? Hadn't it flooded from Britton's Neck to Conway many a time and left the air laden with mosquitoes and gnats that even DDT could not control?

Who would Marty become while he was in Korea? If he was lucky enough to be sent to the China Seas, would he ever be just Marty again? No, he would never again be Moe's Marty that he could talk to about anything and everything. He would return world wise. He would have seen other people and how they live. Maybe he would see how normal people live and learn how he could also have a normal life out there somewhere off from the back side of Giles Bay. Marty was smart and knew how to survive in the real world. You could put him in a doorless room, and he'd build a house around it and find a thousand ways to get out. Some people, like himself, knew theories that had been set in motion before time, but it was the Martys of the world that kept the real world in gear. Would Marty come back to Britton's Neck and be beyond the small focus of Moe Lackey? Would be have become a thinker and be able to see through the veneer of Moe Lackey?

Moe thought back to the fall evening back when he and Marty were about thirteen or fourteen. A tent revival was being held by the Old Neck Missionary Baptist Church in the field down on Highway 378 where years later Blakely Warren, after hearing that a local boy had taken up doctoring in the Neck, would return with big city ideas to open the first stop-and-go restaurant in the triangle made by the two highways, 908 and 378. On that fall evening there had been only sawdust covering the sand, and poles holding up the green canvas tent. Folding wood-slat chairs had been set up in two sections of each side under the tent leaving an aisle between. The aisle led up to an altar, a platform of about fifteen feet long by eight feet deep. On the right side was an upright piano, and in the center was a rough wood pulpit.

Violet Lackey would have felt insulted if anyone had invited her to a tent meeting. "Don't you know I am Episcopalian?" she would have fumed, projecting her chin to better look down her nose at the inviter. "And I'll remain Episcopalian till my dying day!" She would have dared a son of hers to participate in any local religious activity. It had been Moe who enticed Marty to go. The plan was that Marty would borrow Uncle Harold's Ford truck after his uncle drank himself into his nightly stupor. Marty would wait for Moe behind the AME church lot on Highway 908 near the mansion. Moe would sneak out and meet him there. Neither of the boys was in any way religious, but Moe was driven by curiosity. He wanted to see firsthand what these local people did under the tent since he had grown up automatically accompanying his mother to Georgetown for the stiff, starched shirt services he had to endure and felt she never really enjoyed either.

Moe ran like the devil through the bushes and tall pines between the mansion and the clearing where the colored people were going to build a church someday. There sat Marty barely tall enough to see over the steering wheel of his uncle Harold's '42 Ford truck, designed and built before the Ford dynasty troubles started—before the death of Edsel Ford and the government's pull for Ford to make vehicles for the war.

Marty shifted gears with more confidence than was necessary. He swung the truck in among the trees away from the tent meeting and parked it. They crossed Highway 378 and walked to the tarp where people were already singing. They entered at the rear of the tent. An electric light bulb hung from an extension cord down from the center of the tent's ceiling. As their vision adjusted, they scanned the crowd. Several rows of young people from school sat in the back. A few kids were sitting with their parents closer to the front.

The preacher hollered another hymn, *Are You Washed in the Blood. Are your garments spotless? Are they white as snow? Are you washed in the blood of the lamb?* The paradoxical words surely made little sense to Marty, who had never been to church except on the day of his grandfather Price's funeral. He didn't even try to comprehend them, but to Moe the distant cadence was familiar. The congregation gustily sang out the words then sat down, and the offering baskets were passed around. Two men took to each side of the aisles and passed straw baskets from row to row. The basket came by Moe. He winked at Marty and took it with his palm down and his fingers over the side. After the basket had passed, Moe showed him a quarter he had managed to take up undetected. Marty shook his head and, for some reason, wished Moe had not done that. And for some reason Moe thought Marty would be pleased with his craftiness, but sensed he wasn't.

The preacher began preaching softly after a fervent prayer in which his voice rose to pitches higher and higher alternately with levels lower and lower consumed with great passion. The prayer finished, the preacher started off again like a Model T going down the road, slowly, then picking up speed, then revving the motor time and time again. Preacher Scarborough had wide cheeks like a bulldog and silvery white hair parted on the side and combed neatly down to the sides of his round head. He wore a plain black tie and a black suit with full trousers, and as he preached, he paced and panted like a bull from side to side of the platform, often going down on one knee. The most interesting characteristic of Preacher Scarborough was the artful performance of delivery—his voice. His voice rose higher and louder as he said "The Lord" with the "Lord is going to, is going to, is going to, come down, come down, come down and smi—" (higher and higher) "–te the people, the people, the people of this" (blast out) "sinful generation. Yeah. He's—" He repeated this rhythm throughout his impassioned sermon, but somehow his eyes seemed to fall on Moe Lackey with a familiar fear.

Every sentence was delivered the same way for a while. Men shouted out louder and louder, "That's right!" and "Amen, Brother Preacher," "Praise the Lord," and "Have mercy, Jesus!" Then a woman started holding up her hands. Then she started shaking all over and babbling loudly and incoherently. She continued shaking and babbling. In another section of the tent, a woman started doing the same heated dance. Then another and another started the shaking and babbling. This was getting the preacher very excited, and he seemed to glance back at Moe to see if he had noticed the effectiveness of his sermon. He came down from the platform as if he were in a trance. He was shouting out his sermon with the interspersed phrases of babble while he marched down the aisle looking straight in the faces of the people.

He marched a little farther down the aisle each time and then he would pivot and return to the pulpit. One or two of the men, dressed in overalls, went down front moving spasmodically and moved around and then fell in a heap near the platform. Others followed until almost everyone was participating in the pathos, except Moe and Marty and a few more of the younger set that tried to stifle giggles behind their hands, but their eyes told that they were fearful. Some of the women had now fallen over as if exhausted. Moe elbowed Marty time and time again until they noticed that Preacher Scarborough seemed to have set his eyes on them and that the next time he marched down the aisle, he would be in their faces. As he now pivoted and began his march back toward the front, Moe pulled on Marty's sleeve, and the two boys ducked down under the tarpaulin and moved quickly to the darkness outside. As soon as they were about ten feet away from the tent, they ran as fast as they could in the soft sand, laughing so hard they could hardly see their way back to the truck.

Moe, pausing in his laughter and kicking his feet to the floorboard, turned to Marty, "Wait. This night. We need to do something that makes it special, so it'll always be like reaching a plateau. I know the perfect thing we should do." He pulled his Swiss Army knife from his pants' pocket. "Blood. It's always been about blood. Back there in the tent. They sang about blood, didn't they? So blood is the way we will make this night special. We will both shed blood. Mix it. Blood kin, like brothers, you see?"

Marty chuckled. "Yeah, brothers."

"Now, we each will cut our left finger next to the little finger and mix the blood together. But we need us some words to make it legal like. I know. What about—*With this blood which I give you, I voluntarily become your closest next of kin, your brother*—what about that?"

"Okay. Let's do it."

Moe slide the blade across his ring finger and watched as the blood came up in a huge drop. He then handed the knife to Marty who did the same. Then they looked at each other. Moe, solemnly, though Marty was trying to hold back a snicker.

"Say it with me—with this blood," Moe said.

"With this blood," Marty repeated.

"Which I give you."

"Which I give you."

"I voluntarily become your closest next of kin," said Moe.

Marty repeated it.

"Your brother."

"Your brother," Marty said obediently.

"Then we seal it with a kiss," said Moe.

"I don't know about that."

"It's just for the ceremony of it, okay?"

The next day they saw in the halls and classrooms the same teenagers from the night before and noticed that the young people did not appear any holier than usual—even after seeing their parents transported into a realm of physical contortion and spiritual elevation. The kids, themselves, still looked and acted like everyone else. Moe and Marty wondered if those teenagers looked at them and thought the same thing.

Now, four or five years later, with Marty heading out into the world of the United States Army and Korea, would the tie be strong enough to pull them back together as they had been when they became brothers in blood?

Chapter Nine

Money will buy you a pretty good dog,
but it won't buy the wag of his tail.
Henry Wheeler Shaw

War was building up. After July 1950 and the news that Communist troops from the north had plowed into the southern region of Korea, the United Nations, in its very early years, felt a responsibility to act. Here it was that Northern Korea was bullying, and a country cannot do that and get away with it. But the Communists didn't listen and didn't say, "Oh, we didn't know. Please excuse us. It won't happen again." No. They ignored the polite talks. The polite talks turned into commands that had to be backed up. North Korea didn't listen at all but kept on taking over. Sixteen of the countries that had elected to join in the project to unite the nations sent in their young men soldiers. About forty-one countries sent supplies and food. The United States sent thousands of its young men soldiers to help defend the country and millions of dollars for the families of the civilians from South Korea who had already been killed.

Japan had controlled Korea since 1895, but after World War II—1939 until 1945—in fact, Russia had occupied North Korea. Ironically, the United Nations was organized in the fall of the year the war ended (October of 1945), by a group of countries that opposed Germany, Japan, and Italy. These countries had sent representatives to San Francisco in April of 1945 to plan this organization. Fifty nations signed on to the ideal to wipe out war forever. They used the Bible verse that said, "Let us beat swords into plowshares," from Isaiah 2:4, which says "He shall judge between the nations, and shall decide disputes for many peoples; and they shall beat their swords into plowshares, and their spears into pruning hooks; nation shall not lift up sword against nation, neither shall they learn war anymore" (ESV) to express the ideal of world peace and human dignity. It would have been well for the founders to include the next verse, "O house of Jacob, come, let us walk in the light of the Lord" (Isaiah 2:5, ESV).

The second irony was that the Russians made a gift, a statue by their great sculptor, Yevgeny Vuchetich, which depicted this grand notion. The artwork was placed at the United Nations headquarters in New York City. High-sounding verbiage and power to mere men, but can mere mortals achieve such peace? History quickly reveals men in their own power cannot. But man is bent on power. Man has the desire to become like God since only God really has ultimate power. Man is in a state of constant erosion by the diseases of greed, lust, luxury, all borne from the germ of power, a virus that will only be controlled, never eradicated, by the transfer of knowledge that there is only one non-tarnishing, non-decaying, non-weakening power, and that is God. And all the higher rationalization of man will never change that fact. God is God and man is man.

People who know the Bible hold to the knowledge that God sent Jesus in the form of man once and once only for a special purpose, to save mankind from the sin he, man, had created in the first garden home of Eden. The job being done, Jesus crucified to redeem mankind, he ascended to heaven and would never have to become like man again. But, an important notion to keep in mind is this: Man would never become God. Neither is man a little God. But Satan, who was a darling to God while in heaven, tried to prove he was as good as God, and got himself kicked out of heaven, he and his little demons. Since then, they wander the earth creating war in big places of prominence and little places of no-account. And still, anywhere he can get a toehold, Satan is there in disguise to tear down, to thwart, to contort, to ruin, and to bring death.

In July of 1950, the newest newspaper, the *Myrtle Beach Sun*, and the *Myrtle Beach News*, a local weekly newspaper begun by two brothers-in-law in 1935 (and both destined to merge in 1961 to become *The Sun News* of Myrtle Beach) had front-page stories of soldiers marching though the imaginary line called the thirty-eighth parallel. The 38th Parallel would never again be spoken without conjuring up thoughts of Seoul, South Korea, the Yellow Sea, the Sea of Japan, regardless of the fact that to all Koreans, the imaginary line did not make a hill of beans difference. Both sections of Korea, North and South, wanted all of the tiny country. President Truman sent an order for air and naval forces to move toward Korea. Within days the same order was sent to ground forces. Congress okayed Truman's orders without formally declaring the action a war. (Remember, war was out. Peace was supposed to reign now.)

After the North Koreans captured Seoul, American

troops began fireworks. It was July 5 on Osan, thirty miles south of Seoul. General Douglas MacArthur was leading the Americans. On a small piece of peninsula, in a short period of time, lives, which were not lost, were changed forever, destinies declared.

Marty was shipped out before the year was over. He had few regrets about leaving Britton's Neck and his home back of Giles Bay. He was ready to fight for a good cause—he'd been fighting all of his life yet not knowing why. He had lived his life thus far with a chronic vacancy. He looked around the bus that was taking them to the coast. Most of the boys seemed to be doing the same thing he was doing—thinking their own private thoughts. He wanted to say something to one or two of the guys who looked especially homesick, but why should he? He was likely to get a "Leave me alone and mind your own business" or "What would a person like you know about it?" He kept his thoughts and words to himself.

What he felt now and then was a poignant emptiness when he thought of Moe and his mother.

Back home, another war was building up. For Marty's mother Polly, nothing in the world could interest her. It was as if she had built a concrete wall around her mind and her heart. No news, no beauty, no individual could make a scratch on it. She would continue going through the motions of life, but without Marty around, she was apt to forget some mundane phases, like eating or sleeping or bathing. A few times in the past, he had had to prod her to do one or the other of these activities that most people have a compulsion to do.

Then, for Marty, there was no time to think. Listen hard, follow orders fast. Try to stay alive. One moment, one half a moment, one quarter of a moment, one tenth of a moment was all it took to die if you were not careful. Besides constantly stretching his mind to be alert so as not to get blown to bits by the enemy, he found he had to also be on guard against the other GIs who could not resist trying to dominate him because of his diminutive size.

One day while showering, a group of guys began getting wilder and wilder in their vivid demoralizing chatter in the open showers around him. Marty realized that even though they were "cutting the fool," as people in Britton's Neck would say, there was a serious possibility that they may indeed carry out what they were laughing about. He shuttered and clinched his teeth. Steam shielded his view, but he tried to visualize how he could defend himself if it came to that. He only had this bar of soap. He did have a razor and razor blades but not with him right now. He would have to come prepared from now on.

The attack came sooner than he expected. Before he could devise a plan of action, several of the men surrounded him, laughing and catcalling, holding him down under the steady stream of hot water. Kicking and yelling until one of the men stuck the bar of soap in his mouth, Marty gave way to a rage that was beyond any he had ever known. But the surge of strength was not enough to resist all the rough hands and fingers probing and pulling and desecrating his flesh. Just as quickly, the assault was over, and he lay limply on his belly with his face in the pool of soapy water draining away from him.

"It was all in fun, Price," one of them said.

He avoided their eyes and faces from that time on. He

avoided their voices. He tried to avoid feeling altogether. He thought of his rage. A human has an internal rage that comes into effect to fight off the enemy if necessary. He had felt his surge of rage come and reach its limit, but it had not been strong enough to protect him. He had maximized his fury, but it still was not enough. Would his rage ever be enough to defend himself or his own against the evil in this world? Having this knowledge that he lacked the ultimate power against another attack, he considered running away. His simmering madness made him an animal that had been raised free but was now trapped, caged. But somehow, someway, he had to be free again.

Uncle Harold would be disgraced and never forgive Marty if he went AWOL. Would he ever be able to look at his mother, or Moe, or anyone, again without something in his demeanor revealing a telltale sign that he had been defiled? He was an insect in a canister. He was a cricket in a bait bucket. His mind raced over the ceiling of his sleeping quarters until his eyes hurt. His stomach began to cramp at all hours of the day and night until he had to puke. He often felt dizzy just having to strip for showers. His chest felt like a horse had kicked him. Food no longer had any taste. Even the texture of food on his tongue made him wheezy. He knew if he swallowed, it would come back. The mess hall cooks had always picked on him because of his ferocious appetite. Now they riddled him when they saw him dump his tray of food untouched.

He received letters from his mother twice a week, but he was barely able to answer them.

Chapter Ten

Make money, money by fair means if you can,
if not, but any means money.

Horace

The letters, which had come every other week for twenty-four months even if they were fragmented and simple and to the point, or nothing much at all, now only trickled home, and then stopped altogether. Polly had put each one of the treasures in the cloth-covered Havana cigar box she had rescued from the school wastebasket in Mrs. Rogers' classroom.

Mrs. Rogers was the brand new third grade teacher and had probably spent most of her summer making things like the box for her classroom. The box had been meticulously covered with a yellow calico material under which she had stuffed cotton batting. She had carefully glued the fabric to the inside and edges of the box. Polly began to feel guilty as if she had stolen something by removing the box from the trash can. Maybe the teacher didn't actually intend to throw the box away. Maybe it accidently fell into the trash. The teacher surely wouldn't have taken all that time and trouble to cover it and then discard it. Polly knew she would have to do the right thing and ask. She took it to the teacher's classroom after school.

"Mrs. Rogers?" she rapped on the door even though it was ajar. The young teacher, who was at her desk, quickly straightened her back and with both palms wiped her cheeks.

"Oh, 'cuse me. I'm sorry," Polly said, thinking that probably she and her husband, who also taught at the school, must have had a lovers' quarrel since they had been married only a short while.

"It's okay. What is it, Mrs. Price?"

"You must have left this box somewhere, and somehow it got put in the wastepaper basket. I saw your name on the inside. It's such a pretty box that I knew you'd want it back."

"No. I threw it away. It's no good."

"Do you mind terribly if I keep it?" Polly was trying not to notice the wet eyelashes.

"Course not. If there's anything in this room you want, you can have it too." There was sharpness in her voice Polly had never noticed before. Something had happened, and Polly, uncertain what she should do, decided since she was not quite equal to this young, educated, and refined woman, would walk away from the matter.

"No ma'am. I was just wondering about the box. Thank you. It's done up so good it'll be perfect to keep my son's letters in. He's in Korea."

An explosion of emotion erupted from the young woman. Agonized groaning and tears began. She beat her fists on her desk and kicked her feet.

"Mrs. Rogers?" Polly looked around, wishing someone would walk into the room—someone who would know what to do—someone to take charge, so she could slip out quietly, anonymously. She started to leave anyway.

"Oh!" the woman cried with fresh agony.

Polly was compelled to take a step toward the teacher. "Mrs. Rogers, what'n the world?"

"My husband. They sent him a letter. He's been drafted. He's got to go! We just got married this summer. I'll have to move back to Virginia and live with his parents. We just got married and got a duplex apartment. And Christmas coming. Oh—" She was overcome again with tears.

"That's the awfullest thing I ever heard," Polly heard herself say, trying to comfort the girl. "He probably won't be gone long. My boy says it looks like, from what MacArthur says, they'll be home 'fore next summer."

"But why me? Why us? We just got married!"

"Things just happen like that sometimes." Polly could think of nothing else to say to this twenty-something year old educated teacher. Quietly, with the yellow calico-covered vault in her hand, Polly slipped out into the hallway to go home.

She opened the box to fondle the letters. She could not help noticing the difference in Marty's handwriting in his last letters. He was never much for reading and writing. He never had made his letters neat—never had written level on the line. Some words he'd write small, and some he'd write large, but she'd never had any trouble making out his writing. Her writing was not perfect either. But in his last letters, his handwriting was either dark, as if he was bearing down with a lot of pressure, or so light she could hardly see it. Maybe Marty was writing while being shifted around from place to place. Harold had talked about trying to write letters while being stuck in foxholes for days—whole companies of men having to stay for days and nights in a trench, and how irritable men could get. No way for a human being to have to live, especially a young eighteen, nineteen-year-old. Marty had never mentioned foxholes. He usually wrote brief descriptions of the new sights he and the men had seen. He used to ask about Harold and Blanche, but he never asked about anything or anyone anymore. She would like to be able to discuss such thoughts as these foxholes with Harold. Did they have them in Korea? But Blanche was often working rotation.

Blanche worked at the Marion Telephone Company. The job, which Blanche took as soon as she graduated, turned out to be one of the best things Blanche had ever done because it was one of the few job opportunities for Britton's Neck young people other than working in the tobacco fields of Marion County. The telephone company was an ambitious enterprising adventure that many people in Britton's Neck thought could not and would not work. But not Winston and Nadine. They thought whatever Blanche did would work out in the end because she was the smart one. Blanche herself knew she would never be a tobacco farmer's wife. Besides, maybe she could help provide a better living not only for herself but also for her sister Polly and the apple of her eye, little Marty, who lived in the little sharecropper shack beside them. She had no intention ever of going away to college and leaving them. Her parents had built a wall between the two houses that only Blanche could transcend. She had never loved another human being as much as she loved Polly's baby. As he grew, he constantly amazed her with his little boy personality. It was for certain he would be the smartest child the world had ever had to reckon with.

That was her mindset until little Marty entered first grade. Then she learned that teachers could be prejudiced against a helpless, innocent child. She was outraged when Marty's grades in school were even worse than her older sister's had been. She had always been convinced that Polly did not try to learn. But Marty, he was already as smart as a whip. It had to be the teachers' fault that his grades and his work were not the top in his class. Teachers got their feet wet at Britton's Neck school, and then went on to town schools; they came and went like the wind. However, there were some locals who had taught both Polly and herself, and she never dreamed they could hold the child back because he had no father. Blanche used one tactic after another to compensate for Marty's failures, but nothing brought him closer to the top of his class like she had always been and where she felt Marty should be. Gradually, she rationalized that school was a detriment to Marty and encouraged him to stop paying attention to the teachers. He should not take their condemnation seriously. Marty did not need his aunt's permission to ignore the lectures of his boring teachers. It was easy for him to block out their questions, lessons, and reprimands.

As the years progressed, the telephone company caught on and expanded, and Blanche had to devote more and more time and energy to her work. She became a supervisor and then a district manager. Some weeks, she realized guiltily, she had not spent any time at all with Marty nor had she thought much of the little fellow. Somewhere in time past, before she was essential to the growth of the telephone company, she had briefly thought she would like to have children, and she had married Harold, a worthy catch, a respected member of

Britton's Neck and Marion County society such as it was.

Very shortly afterwards, Blanche discovered that marriage was only a self-perpetuating myth. She had not found whatever it was that would cause a woman to risk her respectability to run off to the river on a moonlit night. After she stood before a justice of the peace at the Marion County Courthouse and said, "I do," and heard Harold repeat it, she tried to conjure up such an emotion. Often, in the beginning stages of her and Harold's marriage, she mused that perhaps one day she would develop passions as strong as Polly's must have been to make her run down to the river to meet someone she scarcely knew.

But now, she was beginning to think perhaps it was only Polly's simplemindedness that had caused her to do such a thing after all. Nothing Blanche ever felt came close to that kind of feeling, especially as she climbed into bed beside his thin frame and allowed him, smelling like cigarettes and Jim Beam, to press his scrawny body against hers. Her mind found some phrases she imagined a bride would say, and she breathed her breath into the phrases, hoping they sounded believable. In a few weeks she found she didn't need to pretend. Harold did not and would not know the difference anyway whether she meant any of the phrases. She noticed more and more of his Jim Beam breath. When she started to have a rotation shift at the telephone company, both of them were relieved.

Winston and Nadine, though they had excommunicated Polly as soon as morning sickness began, never openly expressed emotion. Winston felt that moving Polly into the sharecropper's house while she was growing in size with the fatherless baby would give plausibility to the husband in the

Army story. They made sure she had a roof over her head and food to eat but that was all. They had considered asking Nadine's sister Thelma and her husband Louis who lived in Little River to let Polly stay out the time with them, but Winston concluded: Polly has made her bed; now let her lie in it. With the absence of their parental support, Blanche was the only one who came anywhere close to overseeing her sister.

Winston Price gradually seemed to dry up from the inside out after Polly's public shame—first his heart, then his stomach, and then his limbs. The stroke that took his speech also drew up his right hand and arm never to swing a hammer again or place a crosstree over a mule's head or yank out a handful of Nadine's hair before pulling her gown up. Nadine listened to the doctor say that Winston would receive proper care in the state hospital in Columbia. In fact, that was just the place he needed to be. But even after signing the papers and leaving the tiny office, she was not sure she was doing the right thing. These people looked crazy, and just looking at them sent a shiver through her. The doctors assured her that even though she was two and a half hours away, if they needed her, they would call her daughter Blanche at the telephone company. She could come every chance she had to visit Winston. Nadine gradually began to enjoy a sense of liberation from Winston's blows when something did not please him, but something inside made her hope he was still being fed three times a day and bathed at least once a week or so and treated decently.

Winston had never had anything to do with the little fellow, but Nadine knew this child, a man-child, would carry on something that had been associated with her parents and their parents before them. She had known it the night he was born, and she examined him after Lula handed him to her. There on the baby's left buttocks was the mark—the strawberry. It had skipped every other generation. She felt the back of her upper right leg. That was hers—the one claim that made her the favored grandchild of her mother's parents.

"You've got your grandfather's strawberry," her grandmother and mother had always told her. There on Pauline's screaming baby was the one thing that would create a redeeming quality, something in her heart that couldn't be denied, something akin to pride in Nadine's heart even if he was fatherless. He may be fatherless, but he was not family-less. He belonged to the Jernigan line that had come to America on the ship from Aire, Scotland. Often as she sat in the porch rocker, she could not stop her eyes from staring at the sharecropper's house. She thought of the words passed down from her grandmother, "You're Scotch and don't you ever forget it. My mother used to tell me of the Jernigan's journey to the shores of America. They was strong and fierce fighters, and that's the onliest way they coulda made it in the new world."

Marty was seven years old when his elusive granddaddy, whom he feared more than anything else in the world, went away. He had always felt his presence if he happened to cross any bit of the yard even if his grandfather was not there. There had been very few times when he and Polly came to the big house. Now since his granddaddy was gone, his grandma had sent for him to come eat supper with her. The Jernigan blood in her was stirring. She had felt the strawberry itching and knew that her dead kin were calling to her from their graves. Ancestors were telling her that the blood of the child is thicker than blood of a mate. Winston Price had cut off his daughter and her child while he was alive, now she knew she wouldn't have too many more years herself to try to build some bridges. It was hard to look into his miniature face without thinking of the shame they had tried to hide, but who amongst us can throw a stone, she reasoned.

The short walk to the big house from the wood frame house with its one big room and a small bedroom off to one side where he and his Mama lived seemed to call for him to muster up some courage. As he passed Blanche and Harold's house, a small considerably new brick house with a cardinal bird design in the screen door, he was distracted by every grasshopper and had to see if he could catch one.

The yard was brushed clean as his mama's own bare plank floor. No leaf, no blade of grass, no chicken manure—Lula had swept the yards until he could not even leave a footprint. There was a sound coming from the house. He stood looking at the long side porch with the pump shelf and pump and the narrow shelf with the dipper and several glasses, amber tinted from rust, turned upside down.

The sound he heard was his grandmother's voice, "Lula, the little fellow may be scared."

"Yas'um. I 'speck he gwine be scared a bit."

"Now, don't go upsetting him with your tales."

"Yas'um. I try not to. He think the place be haunted by Mr. Winston."

"Sometimes I think it is myself," she said, looking at the dark wooden walls that had never soaked in a drop of paint.

There were two doors leading into the house from the porch, one into the hall and the other into the kitchen. The straw broom Lula used for sweeping the yards leaned against the wall of the house. Inside the hall, there to the left was the door to a room that used to be Polly and Blanche's. An iron bedstead with a chenille bedspread on the bed dominated the little room. One little table and one straight back chair sat in the corner. A closet and a fireplace were on the opposite wall. An oval, multicolored crocheted rug lay beside the bed on the pine wood floor.

He went into the door straight up from the porch steps into the kitchen with its linoleum rug with the ridges of the floorboards underneath imprinted on it. It felt cool to sway his bare feet across the linoleum. There on the left was the fireplace and a cook stove in front of it. A kettle of water sat on the stove. There was a window behind the table. A cloth covered whatever was on the table—the sugar bowl, salt and peppershakers, a little bottle of pepper vinegar, and the bread bowl of morning biscuits. A double flue of the fireplace had once served both of the rooms, the kitchen and the middle room, a bedroom. Now the kitchen fireplace was never used, but in the middle room where Grandma Nadine slept, the fireplace was the only source of heat. A door led from the kitchen to the middle room and out to the hall. On the opposite side of the hall were two more rooms. Besides the kitchen and Grandma's room on the right side was a big living room. It too had a fireplace. The hall ended with the wide front door with the top half glass pane etched designs with vines and intricate flowers surrounding an oval that had the single letter *P* etched in the middle. Tall narrow windows flanked the door.

"We'll eat us a bite of supper. Are you hungry?" his grandma asked Marty as she dipped from a black iron kettle a spoonful of yellow grits. She spooned red tomatoes out of an iron skillet onto the grits and placed a fat biscuit on the side. He watched her fix her plate and sit. Nadine started to bow her head. "Your ma makes sure you say grace, don't she, boy?"

"Some times," he said, not sure of what she was talking about.

Nadine said the blessing and stirred her tomatoes and grits. "Go ahead and eat."

"Them biscuits are good."

Nadine handed a bowl over and lifted back the dishtowel revealing two more biscuits. Then she pushed over to his plate a syrup jar with a spout. She watched as he poured the syrup over the film left by the grits and tomatoes and began sopping the plate clean.

Condensing seven years and two hundred years of Jernigan history into one evening would not work. It would take time. But Nadine Price would not be given that luxury. What she didn't know was that an aneurism was hiding itself on her brain like a time bomb. Before Christmas they would find her beside her rocking chair on the floor, one hand on her head, the other, blue and outstretched, her knees pulled up in a fetal position. She had just turned forty-six years old.

Polly wanted to talk to Harold about foxholes in Korea—were there any that the soldiers had to stay in during battles like he had had to during World War II? Besides, for seven years she had not been alone in this house. Marty was always right there, and she was always talking to him without actually voicing her words. Polly walked out into the summer evening. A breeze blew off the river to cool the bay region.

She wrapped her arms around her bosom and looked up at the sky. The evening star wasn't out yet. Just a breeze. She stepped off the rickety stoop and across the bare yard, not noticing that a piece of the gray Spanish moss dangling from a low hanging branch of the live oak tree had become entangled in her curly red hair.

"Blanche? Harold?" she called as she opened the side door to their kitchen, modern with running water over a white enamel sink. There in the deep sink were several crooked neck yellow squash about the size of a baby bottle. Sand was caked on the bottom sides along with the brown stems. It would not take a minute to wash up the squash and place them in the refrigerator. Harold must have pulled them as he walked through the garden.

Just then she heard a groan coming from the bedroom. The house had three other small rooms beside the kitchen. Leaving the kitchen, she walked into a living room. To the side was the short hall that led to two small bedrooms and one bathroom. Like a child, Polly walked toward the sound. There lay Harold in nothing but his underwear on top of the bedspread. The window was up and the slight breeze blew the curtain. Each time the curtain floated across his bare chest, he groaned. His bottle of Jim Beam was on the nightstand under the lamp that had not been turned on.

"Blanche," she called, not knowing why. She already knew Harold was alone. She turned to go.

"Come here," he moaned from the bed. "Come here, Polly, please," he said pitifully. She stepped toward him, and he swung his long legs off the bed and looked at her crazily. "You have something in your hair," he said after a minute and reached for the moss. The breeze blew the curtain behind him, distracting her momentarily.

His long arms pulled her to him, and for a brief second, she did not know if she were Polly, Blanche, or Harold, nor was she cognizant of where she was or why she was there. His arms were strong and pulled her into his face, and his alcoholic breath came from his fiery hot lips. He pulled her down on top of him, and his hands lifted her dress. She could hardly breathe. Her air was cut off from her though she felt the breeze coming from the river. Only his pungent breath was keeping her lungs from collapsing. He turned her over so that his weight pressed her down, and his hands groped her in different places. His mouth was on hers so that she could not speak. A volcano was erupting inside her, and she had no time to think outside of the fire that kept rising, and the river's breeze that kept blowing through the open window. Then as suddenly as a raging bull can forget what he was attacking, Harold fell back against the pillow and groaned loudly. "Leave me alone, Polly. Leave me alone!"

She pushed free of his leg crosswise hers and pulled her crumpled dress down as she groped blindly from the room. She would never know if Harold ever remembered that night or not; it was never spoken of by either of them. One thing was certain however—her womanhood, even though it suffered from disuse, was not dead.

Chapter Eleven

Business, you know, may bring money,
but friendship hardly ever does.
Jane Austen

Going through the chow line, Marty could often hear a tease from a direction to which he would not look. "Strawberry," some GI from his company would have said along with a low whistle. The rage was building in his ears to a point he could hardly see. He would not eat today. If he was walking past mud-walled huts with thatched roofs and rice paddies or throwing grenades, he seldom heard the nickname he'd been tagged since the shower attack, but as soon as there were safe times when the men were not concerned with staying alive, he would hear them, like wolves who had tasted blood and now sniffed the air continually searching for more. He tried to sit by himself away from others, but that was impossible with the mess hall full of men. He spoke only when spoken to and then with fragmented answers unless he was talking to an officer. He elaborated on nothing.

Bending over the disabled vehicle, Marty heard the wolf whistle and then, "Hi ya, Strawberry, wanna take a shower?" His grip on the wrench tightened until his knuckles turned white. He whirled, and as he did, he lifted the wrench hoping to expel as much force as necessary to silence the speaker.

Before him with his head slightly lowered was 1st Lt. Caravich, with a sideways smirk on his long, narrow, acne-riddled face. His hat was cradled in his muscular left arm at the elbow, leaving his blond bush cut head exposed. His arms were covered with blond hair. He was more than a foot taller than Marty and looked to be made of steel. He was the camp's best arm wrestler and the platoon's heavy weight champion.

"You want to show me the wrench? I see," he teased. "You wouldn't want to take a shower now, would you? Since those damn Communists fled Pyong Yang, things have been a little boring around here, don't you think?"

"I've got work to do," muttered Marty and turned.

"PFC Price, you will salute a superior before turning your back."

Once again, Marty's hand gripped the wrench, but he sighed, lifted his hand in a salute and quickly turned back to the motor.

"Bye, bye, Strawberry."

One thing and one thing only kept Marty sane—his work—the sight of an engine, the smell of oil, the sound of motors, and the touch of tools in his hands. *Yet he knew that to stay sane, he must get out of this division.* He would have to apply for artillery. He had to get into a unit where he could be engaged in action with the enemy instead of his own men. His request was met as if he were a culprit. No complaints had been filed against PFC Price. He had done satisfactory work although of late, he had several sick days.

"How do you think you're going to transfer to an artillery battalion if you can't cut it in tank battalion," Sgt. Flynn snapped but waited on Marty's answer.

"Sergeant, Sir, I have worked on motors all my life back home, and when I get back home, I'll work on motors for the rest of my life. While I'm serving, Sir, I want to see action and make a difference." He had overheard another soldier say that commenting on making a difference by serving in combat went over well with officers. He had rehearsed his speech over and over in his mind.

Chapter Twelve

A man is usually more careful of his money than of his principles.

Oliver Wendell Holmes, Jr.

Mrs. Rogers' husband turned out to be a 4-F due to an allergy to wool used in making military uniforms. He returned and was back in his own classroom, and Mrs. Rogers once again was herself and never mentioned the cigar box though Polly kept thinking she might remember it and ask for it back. Polly thought the young couple must love each other with a fierce devotion by the way Mrs. Rogers had carried on when she thought he would be called into the service. But as she observed the couple on the few times they were together, however, she wondered. How does anyone know if a man and woman really love each other, or how can you measure the amount of love? She had never thought about her parents "loving" each other. Enduring, surviving, tolerating, yes—but loving?

She could not imagine either of her parents acting any differently with anyone else. Blanche and Harold—what was the ingredient that held these two in marriage? Theirs seemed to be the same situation. She had grown up thinking Blanche, who was the feminine, softened, and sensible one would make a wise decision when it came to marriage like she had always made about everything else. Like the telephone company—in spite of everyone's advice, Blanche had good judgment in choosing to take a chance with the new enterprise. Wise. Blanche was wise and good fortune smiled on the wise. The only people who did not take to Blanche were the halfway good-looking or the halfway smart ones; these women felt threatened by her. The ugly women and the truly beautiful felt no competition with Blanche. The same way with intelligent people, she had noticed. With men, Blanche was wise. She was businesslike but considerate. Men would never try anything with Blanche, at least, not more than once. She would put them in their place quickly and finally.

The Rogers couple—even though they were young—did not act like they knew each other in public. Maybe that was how decent people were supposed to act—distant and aloof. Mrs. Rogers hung around the female teachers, especially Mrs. Hendricks, several years older, whose husband was also a teacher. Mr. Hendricks was a science teacher and boys' basketball coach. The Hendricks lived across the road from the school in the teacherage that housed two apartments, one upstairs and one down. The downstairs was occupied by the principal and his wife, Mr. and Mrs. Poston. The Hendricks would leave after school, and then he returned for practice, after which he'd drive the ballplayers home since none of them had cars. Polly thought it was odd that the Hendricks often did not even look at each other if they were in the lunchroom at the same time, but they appeared jovial with others. Maybe Mr. Poston had warned married couples never to act like they were married. But it was none of her business anyway, Polly decided.

Christmas came and went, Easter came and went, and the letters from Marty grew stranger and stranger and finally stopped coming altogether. She had begun to worry someone else was writing the letters and signing Marty's name. Maybe he was wounded or missing in action, and they did not want her to know. How could anyone understand how she felt? Simply, no one could. No one could possibly know her unexplainable worries. She did not understand herself.

No one could have ever felt the curiosity concerning life she had felt once, when she was sixteen, that if God did not lift her out of this mistake of a place and let her experience the world and all there was out there somewhere that she would burst wide open or turn inside out. Maybe that's how Marty felt before he got away from Britton's Neck. Could he have experienced the same battle for restraint she had growing up. A realm of questions about intimacy bounced back and forth in her mind as she heard through the walls the condemnations of her father toward her mother then moments later his ranting like a horse for a few minutes. Finally she'd hear his heavy sigh, followed by his snoring. Though she could not have articulated it, she documented it in her mind as a concerto.

No one could have ever known the weight of her curse upon her when she was Marty's age following her stolen moments and facing life alone with a baby growing inside her. No. No one could know how long it took her to conquer her Eve nature. Oftentimes in the early years of Marty's life, she thought she had conquered the wild-horseness in herself and could now live a life of humbleness and servitude, but after sleep, some dawns brought a dread so powerful she could not have forced her feet to move to touch the bare, cold floor if she had not heard the voice calling, "Ma." And that call "Ma" was the only reason she didn't take one last walk to the river and keep walking.

Some sunrises brought emptiness inside her gut that led to questioning *what for? What is life that it is dished out with no regard to justice, fairness? What kind of God would let there be people born too poor while some were born too rich? What kind of God would allow such inequity of life? What kind of God could create a man like Hitler who could cause the entire world to go to war and millions of innocent people blown up before they had ever really lived? And how could God make people like the North Koreans who push and push and push—who kill their own people—why would God let such injustice happen over and over in the world? And how could there be a God who could even care about a common worm like me,* she thought.

If there truly is a God, is he supreme? Or are there other gods too, who play games for people's lives? *If so, then God would say, "Okay, that one is yours" and that person's future would turn out like hers, spurious, empty. But what about Marty's? The true and Almighty God would want to keep Marty. He had a future! He could not be wounded or dead!*

She had to do something! She could not simply sit and wallow in pity. She would go to Violet Lackey on her way home from school today. Violet was older. She was rich. She knew people outside of Britton's Neck. She made things happen when she wanted to—she was sending her son to college, and very few boys from Britton's Neck went away to college.

Where once a chasm of curiosity about the world existed, now there was a raging sea that Polly could not calm. The injustice of life had taken everything from her, and something inside that rage wanted to demand something back. Dare she demand?

Violet Lackey finally stumbled to the door. Her eyes red-rimmed, and her cheeks flushed. "Pauline. I didn't call you. I don't owe you any money." Her words were slurred, and her head twitched. Pauline could guess she was into her wine a bit heavy this afternoon. In this condition, Violet may not be of any use to her in finding out about Marty, but she could not leave without making an attempt. She could fill in the blanks on another day when Violet was sober, but she had to start today.

"Mrs. Violet, I need to talk to you and get your help. I need you to help me. Call somebody you know. Find out about Marty."

"Martin? Is something wrong with Martin? He's not missing in action, is he?" Violet was half drunk, but her words did indicate she understood at least for the time being. "Come in, Pauline."

Polly entered the dark house and was met by the dank smell that pervaded the old mansion as if all the family dead were stuck in one of the side rooms instead of down in Old Georgetown Cemetery with the other Lackey dead or far away in Trinity Episcopal where Violet once said most of her family were buried.

"I just know someum is wrong. I can tell it in my bones."

"Now, Pauline. You've just gotten to the point... this point... " she was searching for the right words to separate her own feelings about Moe, her son, and Polly and her son. "Christmas, we've had a few Christmases, and our boys are not the lads they used to be, underfoot and all. Toys. Christmas toys and such. Candy and fruits. Easter. Dressing 'em up for church... well, if we... . They've grown up and left the coop, so to speak. They are out there in the world." Violet supported herself by leaning heavily on a carved cherry wood Queen Victorian armchair in heavy velvety covered cushions. "Doing the world some good. Someday they'll come home... they will come home to their mothers. They will resume the roles that nature set in pace... place for them, Pauline."

Not to be deterred by Mrs. Violet's tipsy speech, Pauline spoke and hoped she was being heard. "He hasn't written me in months. That don't set right with me, Mrs. Violet. He's not a heavy writer, but since he's been over there, he's wrote me just about every other week till—now the letters—they've stopped altogether."

Looking as if she would topple over at any moment, Violet said, "I'm not sure what I'll be able to learn, but I'll call my cousin, the senator. Tomorrow. Yes, tomorrow," said Violet pressing the back of her hand to her forehead as if filing the directive away for the time being.

Polly was afraid Violet's memory wouldn't last as long as the alcohol content of the wine. "I'll write down his company and address for you to give 'em when you call. I will be indebted to you, Mrs. Violet. Is there some work you need done? I'll be happy to come over tomorrow and do it for you."

She wanted to return to jar Violet's memory, but she left feeling she may have gotten a little closer to Marty. As Polly left, it dawned on her that tomorrow afternoon may find Violet in the same state of intoxication. *I don't blame her*, Polly thought. What has the old woman got anyway? Her son's gone from her too, but at least, he is still within reach, and it was not likely Moe Lackey would ever be found in harm's way.

Polly did not have to be apprehensive for long about Violet's forgetting her pitiful entreaties. The next morning as Polly was peeling the last of the potatoes for the cauldron of vegetable soup to be fed to the two hundred boys and girls, the Cadillac drove up to the lunchroom door, and Mrs. Violet in her pleated shirt and cardigan sweater stepped out and up the steps into the lunchroom.

"Pauline," she said in her usual direct voice, "I spoke with Cousin Elliott Knotts, and he's going to have Washington call to check on Martin. It may take a few days, but as soon as I hear, I'll get you word. After all, our boys are all we have, aren't they?"

Polly was deeply moved. Violet almost never left the mansion. "Well, you must be god-awful busy," said Violet.

Polly felt as if she would give in to tears. She looked up from the basin of brown potato peelings into Violet's rouged and powdered face, "Mrs. Violet, one day I'll repay this favor. You can count on it."

If not a kindred spirit, something akin to it had made Violet respond with urgency to Polly's request. As she backed her car out, her thoughts were of Moe, her own son, who had just left a few days ago to return to the university. While he had been home, he was studying continuously. He was never there at the mansion anymore, spending summers at school away from her. For years, she had detected a growing bond between Moe and Marty, one that shut her out completely. She shivered, shaking her head visibly. There had been another child once, and her leaving had left irreparable damage. And then, Davis gone too, leaving her alone with a son to rear.

There was also something about Pauline Price's simplistic nature that reminded her of the vacuum that had been created by Hazeline's absence.

When Polly turned her gaze back to the pot of potatoes, she noticed the glistening in the sunlight of a fish scale that had dried onto the skin of her inner left arm from the bream she had scaled the night before for her supper. Was this a sign? She thought it must be an omen that Mrs. Violet Lackey's coming to tell her about the call to her relative was a word from God that he was sending hope? Could God be taking matters into his own hands?

Chapter Thirteen

Money is a crazy cab to follow because
after a while, all the cabs look the same.
Sandra R. Pound

He didn't have long to wait until his transfer to Offensive Operations was complete. In May 1952 North Korea began exerting more and more force. Intensified artillery fire was wounding more American soldiers. *Back home to South Carolina* was Marty's thought, when he could think. *One way or another, I've got to get back to South Carolina soon, or I'll never get back.* The umbilical cord had almost been severed to his southern state. In fact, South Carolina seemed to him to have existed in another lifetime. He never saw or heard or smelled anything that made him think of home like some of the guys, who oftentimes made comments like, "Boy, that smell reminds me of so and so back home" or "That sounds just like something back home." Maybe the reminders were due to the fact that the boys making the statements would be going back home again one day. They were still connected to home. They still had a tie to home even though they were thousands of miles away from home. They could just open a door in time and be back sitting in their 1949 sedan or sitting on their front porch watching the cars drive by or going to a theater down on Main Street watching Humphrey Bogart in *Chain Lighting* or *Key Largo*. But no reminders were hitting the memory button in Marty's mind. He had to try to unscramble his brain just searching for who he was anymore. And often he didn't know and couldn't come up with a clue to who in hell he really was anymore.

Chapter Fourteen

I wish it grew on trees, but it takes
hard work to make money.
Jim Cramer

Back on the University of South Carolina campus among over five thousand students was Moe Lackey who had doubled up on all his classes and had private tutoring during the summer instead of going home. What would be the purpose of punishing himself by being in Britton's Neck with no one to talk to? He liked the pressure of being a student. For the past twelve years of school he had aced all subjects without a challenge, but here at the university he had to push himself just to meet all the classes he took. He liked to study while sitting on the grass of the horseshoe where he occasionally could hear the political science students in their strong Democratic arguments debating a Republican issue. The Republican voices were being raised more and more. They spoke their opinions louder and more liberally than they had ever been in South Carolina. The sound of their own voices gave the young rebels raw courage to continue building momentum. It surprised them when they saw that others were listening; they discovered their valid arguments were leading to objectives and agendas.

One person who began listening to these voices was

a slight man, not noticeably tall, who had started out as Superintendent of Education in the peach county of Edgefield in 1929 and then was elected to the South Carolina Senate during the lean years of 1933. This man, who had a passion for patriotism and pretty women, had dutifully dropped his career in 1942 to enlist in the U.S. Army to serve his country in Europe and the Pacific during World War II. He had risked his life more than once and was compensated by having bestowed on him the Bronze Star, Purple Heart, Bronze Arrowhead, and the Legion of Merit upon returning to South Carolina in 1945. He was presently serving as a Democrat Governor of the state but was listening to the young Republican voices. Moe heard the political talk but as an eavesdropper not a participant. He was cognizant that his mother's cousin, whom he hardly knew and had rarely seen, was serving in the US Senate, and that Governor Strom Thurman had campaigned strongly against him.

Moe scribbled notes hastily trying to keep up with Professor Burquist with his mind as well as his pen. He liked to know he understood the brilliant teacher's precepts, and if he didn't, he raised his hand to ask questions. He was totally absorbed in Dr. Burquist lecture on behaviorism and had not even heard someone rap at the door. Burquist nodded toward a student closest to the door. Only when the student soundlessly tugged at his sweater did Moe realize he was being summoned. He was slightly disoriented momentarily at being interrupted while in serious thought. Then his thoughts turned to apprehension when he recognized that it was the college president who had greeted students at freshmen orientation who was waiting for him at the door and leaned toward him and whispered, "Get your books and come with me."

Something tragic must have happened or there was a mix-up in students for the president of the college to summon him personally. As they walked away, Dr. Laurens began, "Moses, are you finding your way around campus sufficiently? I understand you have an unbelievable schedule, taking an exorbitant number of classes. Are you getting on in your studies appropriately?"

Moe knew the guise of pleasantries was a screen for whatever serious and somber earthquake was to follow, but his upbringing in his mother's house forbade his rushing the eminent figure walking beside him. He made an effort to contain himself until the reason for this event was announced. "Let's step in Dean Holland's office, shall we?" Which happened to be the first office on the hall.

He had never been in a professor's office and was surprised that it was small and cramped. Dr. Laurens propped one hip comfortably on the edge of Dean Holland's desk, which was covered with papers and motioned for Moe to have a seat in the only chair in the room besides the desk chair. He observed the cubicle of an office was cluttered with African and Egyptian artifacts and photos. Many of the framed photographs were of the man he assumed to be Dean Holland.

"I guess you are wondering why I called you out of class."

"Yes sir."

"Well, your mother called—she's all right. She isn't sick, but she had some rather bad news she wanted me to give you."

Moe's mind was a total blank. Bad news. If she wasn't dead, what possibly could be bad enough to call the president of the college?

"Your friend Martin Price."

"Marty? No! He's been killed?"

"No, he isn't dead." He held out his arm to touch Moe on the shoulder compassionately at a distance. "He has been wounded in conflict. Your mother has been in contact with the Senator's office—and pardon me—I didn't realize the family connection there. The Senator is having your friend shipped home as soon as possible. Your mother will be in contact. She will let you know when he will be arriving in the states."

Marty. Wounded. Not dead but wounded. How seriously? What had happened? Moe's mind raced. Surely, he knew the possibility existed, but Marty was invulnerable. Marty was too sly and too quick to get in front of enemy fire. He wouldn't have run, but he wouldn't—it must have been a major bombing or something on that order. "Do you have any details, sir?"

"No, Moses, I'm sorry. I talked to your mother myself and tried to remember as much as possible of our conversation, but the Senator's office is going to be in touch with you in a few days. Let me say that my home, my office is open to you, son. Feel free to come in at any time. Would you like to go over now for a few hours to let this sink in?"

"No, sir. I need to get back to class. If you'll excuse me," he extended his hand. He had almost forgotten to thank him. After he left the office, he realized he was tenser than he thought. Instead of returning to class, he started to walk across the horseshoe to his dorm. But instead of going to his room, he continued to walk through Maxey Gregg Park and on toward the mill village of Olympia. He had walked for some time when he reached the South Carolina State Farmers Market. Looking out across the market he knew he was facing east, and if he were a bird, he could fly directly east for about one hundred miles and alit in Britton's Neck. Farmers were here with their bounty. Something about the rum-colored skinned farmers in their wagons and pickup trucks filled with their vegetables and fruits made him feel connected to the farmers back home in Britton's Neck even though all the years when he was at home in Britton's Neck, he felt quite disconnected to them. He turned back.

He had walked farther than he had since he'd been at school. He had no idea that he still had his composition notebook and textbook under his arm. He began his walk back on Olympia Avenue. As he neared Olympian Mills, a whistle blew and the mill hands streamed out of the cotton mill and went toward cars and waiting buses. He saw now why these mill hands were often called lint heads. Fibers, lint, had attached to the workers. They had lint on their shoes, clothes, hair, beards and even some had lint protruding from their nostrils. He stood transfixed looking at the scene unfolding before him: Hundreds of people were streaming from the mill—a gigantic red brick structure with rows and rows of windows and a center clock tower that seemed to reach to the sky. It looked like something straight out of a Charles Dickens novel.

Some of the workers appeared to be full of gaiety and energy while others looked broken and bone weary, especially the women and younger children. He began to feel tired himself. He had walked downhill all the way from campus. Now as he retraced his steps, it was an uphill climb. He had needed to do something extraordinary like Marty would have done. He started slowly and had not gone far when he was about to pass the saltbox house where several of the mill workers were headed. A couple of the men had lunch pails and pulled off their dirty, worn caps as they climbed the steps to the porch. Duplicate half columns of brick and concrete flanked the steps with flowerpots containing summer's end plants. Two girls were already sitting on the concrete steps of the house and pulled their legs close to allow the men to pass. Evidently they had been watching Moe because they waited until he was in earshot,

"Hey, college boy. Come in and have a drink. You look like you could use one."

Ordinarily, he would have pretended he had not heard the girls, but he suddenly felt that to sit and rest for a few minutes before walking back to the dorm was the most sensible thing he could do, and extraordinary, like something Marty would nudge him to do. He turned toward the porch. The girls laughed and looked at each other before jumping up.

"Here let me take your books." He was surprised himself that he was allowing these unfamiliar young women to lead him like a blind man into the dark house. No lights were on, and his eyes had not adjusted to the contrast in bright sunlight to the dark interior. It took several seconds for his eyes to grow accustomed to the inside of the front room where a sofa and several straight chairs faced a dining room. An upright piano was in the living room. "Come sit down by me," one of the girls purred. Then the other pulled him by his arm, saying, "No, sit beside me. What's your name? You're cute." Moe began to think how he'd retell this experience to Marty. Then he remembered Marty had been wounded. He may die. He might even be dead at his moment.

"You said you had a drink?" he mumbled.

"Yeah, sure, let me get you one." She practically ran through the dining room to the kitchen where several people had gone to wash up. She returned with a tall glass about half full of an amber liquid. She deliberately touched his hand when she gave him the drink. When he sipped it, his throat burned like fire. He knew she'd think he was a hick if he coughed. His eyes watered, and his forehead felt as if it would separate from his head. The other girl had turned to a record player and chosen a thirty-three.

"Do you like Kitty Wells? This is her latest recording. Some people say I sound just like her. What do you think?"

"It Wasn't God Who Made Honky-Tonk Angels" whined on the record player and the girl sang along. Moe tried to listen to the words and found he had not much control over his thinking. Before he realized it, he had taken another swallow of the whiskey. It burned his throat but not as much it did at first. He and Marty had slipped whole bottles of his mother's wine many times before, but this stuff was stronger than wine.

"Let me put your books over here, and you and me dance, college boy. You look like you could dance real good."

Moe stood; he was much taller than either of the girls. She placed his hand on her waist and took his left hand. The two girls laughed at his stiff movements, but his awkwardness was ebbing. A mirror over a sideboard showed his reflection though not entirely in focus. His sandy blond hair was neatly combed over his high forehead. His pale skin was slightly darkened by the shadow of a moustache and beard. His shoulders were rounded and not too broad.

"My turn," the other girl cut in. She was rather pretty but more heavy set. Her bangs dangled, almost covering all of one of her eyes. She had large brown eyes and long lashes. Her skin was like cream. "What's your name, or did you tell me?" he asked, feeling more and more at ease as they moved their bodies—though not exactly in rhythm with the guitar and fiddle music and words that Kitty Wells quivered out.

"Alma Dean. What's yours? You've never danced before, have you?"

"People call me Moe but my name is Davis Moses Lackey, III. At your service, and no, I have never danced period."

"The third," they both giggled.

"Where are you from, Moe?" Alma Dean asked. "You ain't from Columbia, are you?"

"No," he sighed, "and there's no point in telling you because you wouldn't have heard of it, and you won't know where it is anyway."

That only increased both girls' curiosity. They started guessing wildly. "Where? Sumter? Florence? Spartanburg? Greenville?" They reminded him either of a mythological story or fairy tale and suddenly the entire incident seemed hilarious, and he began to laugh uncontrollably, letting go of Alma Dean.

"Do you have a public bathroom I could use?" He asked, still laughing.

The girls had looked at each other and laughed along with him. Moe swaggered toward the direction they had pointed. He relieved himself and looked at his face in the medicine cabinet mirror. His face was covered with red splotches, and his eyes were glassy. First—the shocking news of Marty, then the hot sunshine and long walk, now the strong liquor. As he came out of the bathroom, he bumped into a couple of the male mill workers who had entered the house before him. They looked no older than he. They stared stonily at him. Before he could speak, one of them said in a low, gruff voice, "Don't you think it's time you get on back to your classroom, college boy?"

"Yeah," the other added. "You don't want night to fall and catch you down here in Olympia. Things can get purty wild down here. You better start on back before you get locked out of yer dormitory."

"Stay. Dance some more. We was just getting started," the no-name girl pleaded as he headed out the front door.

"Will you promise you'll come back?" Alma Dean said following him out to the sidewalk. She handed him his books he had completely forgotten. A woman's voice from inside called Alma Dean to come help set the table for the boarders.

He willed himself not to stagger as the walked along the uneven sidewalk back to his dormitory.

Chapter Fifteen

If money is your hope for independence
you will never have it.
Henry Ford

Toward the end of the summer, things in Britton's Neck were beginning to change. Suddenly Britton's Neck was getting paved roads. Tar trucks chugged down Highway 908, and the stench of hot tar was in the air day after day. It mattered not one iota that in Charleston, Columbia, Greenville, and Spartanburg, women with agendas were meeting in affluent homes or in college faculty houses to formulate and consolidate the Women's League of Voters for the state of South Carolina. Only one woman in Britton's Neck had gotten wind of such meetings, and she, existing like a lone survivor on an island, lifted her glass of Burgundy and simply toasted, "More power to you." Her call to Elliott Knotts Bradley had momentarily brought a whiff of family memories back to her cousin. Now she must call to thank him on two counts—sending information on Martin Price and the paved roads in Britton's Neck, which would be nice when her son set up his medical practice.

Over on the bay road, Polly felt she would absolutely burst of her own energy one minute, and die of exhaustion the next. She'd go to the worn cloth sofa and lie down. She was used to lying there until time for work the following day. She would be better when school started back and she had work to do, she told herself. She wore a hairnet while at the job, so it didn't matter that her hair was unwashed and uncombed. Her apron covered her dress that often was the same one she'd worn the day before. She hadn't had a monthly menstrual cycle for several years, and recently her bowels seemed to have atrophied also. The mechanics of her anatomy were functioning at a minimum, making it easier for her to omit personal hygiene.

It was a good thing she didn't have to drive anywhere because her car wasn't sounding right. Maybe Marty would be here before Labor Day and the start of another school year, and he could take a look at the motor and fix anything that wasn't working properly. It seemed an eternity since Violet's kin person called Washington, DC, and they had located Martin over in Seoul, Korea, near the Imjin River. He had been wounded, and as soon as possible, he'd be coming home.

The second longest summer of her life felt like a slow motion blister forming on her body. The organ called her heart had already diseased and atrophied and formed a water blister with a thin expanded skin tissue likely to rupture at any moment. The decisive variable was Martin's coming home. If he came before it burst, she might survive. If his coming delayed much longer, the enlargement would burst and drain the remaining life from her limbs. If there were gods exposing her life for all to see, they were surely castings bets in death's favor.

Of course, she felt there was really no actual physical disease, except neglect and self-abuse. She endured.

It was the week before school opening, and she had to check the lunchroom. She had never been the one to order the cans of food, but she had to check to see that it was there and out of the boxes and on the shelves. She had to see that the lunchroom was swept, mopped, and spider webs down from the corners and ceiling. The principal reminded her every year, "They may come to inspect at any moment, and the floors, windows, and kitchen area—everything needs to be spic and span, or we will be in a hellova lot of trouble." Whoever *they* were, she never really knew, and she wasn't sure she'd recognize them if they did show up; therefore, she lived in mortal dread that they would come this year as they had never visited before to her knowledge.

Perspiration soaked her underarms and she felt the drops of sweat trickle down her spine. Usually the gallon cans weren't as heavy, but today, lifting them from the boxes and stacking them on the shelves tired her out more than it ever had before. She pushed the cans in line with the others and stood to a room suddenly gone black. She gripped the shelf. The wave of weakness subsided gradually, and the darkness receded. She had a third of her job to do yet. She better go to Williams' store and get a Coca Cola and pack of nabs and BC Headache Powder.

Shirley was bent over the counter looking at the Sears Roebuck & Company catalog with one of the salesmen. His head was visible through a cloud of smoke, but his words were inaudible as he spoke to Shirley, who continued studying the shoes on the page before her for a second longer before looking up. "Morning, Pauline. Heard from yo boy yet?"

"He's 'posed to be on the way home as soon as he kin

travel's all I know. Worrisome not knowing."

"Imagine so. This woman's only son's overseas—wounded, and we just waiting to get him home," she said to the salesman.

"Is that so?" The salesman turned his attention to Polly, making her feel uncomfortable under his gaze.

The question in Shirley Williams's voice was registered for reasons not entirely of concern, she knew. Shirley kept everyone up to date on everybody else's business, and Marty's had been the lead story since spring.

"You might better give me a BC and a bottle of that Spirits of Ammonia, Shirley."

As Polly left the store, she knew her biography was being repeated for the benefit of the salesman. For five minutes her life was more important to Shirley Williams than the new shoes in Sears catalog or placing her canned goods order with the salesman.

She mixed a teaspoon of the ammonia with water and quickly drank down the burning mixture to settle her lightheadedness. She'd save the BC for later.

Chapter Sixteen

It doesn't matter about money; having it,
not having it. Or having clothes, or not having them.
You're still left alone with yourself in the end.

Billy Idol

Moe's mind grew foggy when he thought of Marty. No more news had come concerning him. Several times Moe had felt he must visit the college president, Dr. Laurens, and ask him to call whomever he had talked to in the first place, but each time he refrained, afraid he'd knock on the door of the two story brick house on the right upper part of the horseshoe and be met by a black butler who'd tell him to get lost or, at least, that students were not allowed in the president's residence. The other reason he did not call on the president and ask for help was that each day he was certain that this would be the day he'd learn something about Marty. He had to hear something soon. In the back of his mind he was alert to hear and react. He considered calling his mother, but in each letter she'd written, she'd said she'd let him know as soon as they heard anything. Her letters also made it more real that Marty must have gotten hurt pretty badly, but she continually reminded him that his studies were his salvation, and he must work doubly hard to achieve the goals to which they aspired, and he was destined to achieve. In her even and graceful handwriting, she'd told him that when Marty did arrive in the states, his aunt Blanche would certainly drive her sister Polly to Columbia to Fort Jackson to bring Marty home, but they might need his assistance and would certainly need the moral support at such a time. Marty's poor mother had barely eked by since he'd joined the Army, which only proved that Martin was all she had to dote on in this life.

Moe walked from the Sloan Building on the northern side of the horseshoe toward the older homes he'd have to pass on his way to his dormitory. He passed Petigru Law Building, the university's newest addition. For a brief second his attention was drawn to something familiar, like seeing a glimpse of a budding fruit that yesterday was a flower. The heavy-set girl with upturned ivory face was talking—rather—listening to one of the law students, who held his books and writing pad nonchalantly under his arm. She kept trying to step away from him, but the tall, dark-haired young man in his tan tweed jacket and yellow tie kept motioning by throwing his chin out and up in a "come closer" exchange while verbally coming on thick with low talk.

Moe had learned not long after arriving at college that the fraternities had an ongoing competition of their conquests with females and published results in a points system. Only once or twice had a reported liaison been challenged, and a mock trial held. Reportedly, one student who claimed a score finally confessed that he had not fully executed.

The girl smiled at the law student, and he reached to put his arm around her shoulder like a wasp encircling its targeted fruit.

"Alma Dean?" Moe asked.

"Well, I'll be a monkey's uncle! I have been over here every day for a solid week looking for you, and now, after meeting Jim, I finally see you."

Jim flinched at hearing her say his name, *Jim*, which apparently was an alias. He looked annoyed that Moe had interrupted his conquest.

Alma Dean, shaking off Jim's arm and running toward Moe, yelled back, "Bye, Jim. Maybe we'll meet up some other time. You'll be a good lawyer. You sure do know how to talk."

She turned her full attention toward Moe and joined him in a stride that had slackened since coming upon the pair.

"You've been coming on campus to see me? Why?"

"Yeah, you're a hard one to find. I don't have that much to do 'cept help ma in the boarding house when I'm not in school. So's I walked over here. It's good exercise."

"Why would you come looking for me?"

"I figured you wouldn't be coming back over to Olympia, and, well, I just wondered what you was like and all. You ran off so quick that night."

"Well, I—"

"It's okay. How are your studies? What do you come to college for anyway? Ha! I mean—you aren't going to be a lawyer, are you?"

"You should be careful talking to the campus boys around here. College boys are too old for you."

"Oh, should I? What are you—a priest?"

"Quite the contrary. You should be wary of me most of all," he said, hoping it came off as a joke.

For a minute, Moe stopped to study her skin, the creamiest he'd ever seen, and wondering how old she actually was.

No girl from Britton's Neck had ivory-colored skin like hers; their years of working in the fields and on the farm had tanned their skin. Of course, his mother's skin was alabaster white because she took extra care to keep it that way by ordering mail order creams and never exposing herself to the sun. Alma Dean's had no lines, no imperfections, but it was not white-white but cream.

"I didn't mean anything by that." She sounded boggled and perhaps embarrassed.

"What?"

"Asking if you was a priest."

Now he knew she was implying something about his sexuality. They looked ahead at the herringbone brickwork path beneath their feet, silent for a few minutes. They were nearly at his dormitory where females were not allowed. "We'd better stop here," he said. For a moment he felt the full force of being awkward. He'd always known he was different, but his differences had been accepted in a community that already knew he was not like them. Now the knowledge of an outsider making the initial discovery of his differentness was totally encapsulating.

She toyed with a section of her gabardine-pleated skirt. "I just meant—" both of them started.

"I was only telling you that some men are not honorable even if they plan to go into honorable professions. They may attempt to take advantage of unsuspecting young women for frivolous means. Even *I* could have such intentions, you never know."

"Well, I'll be a monkey's uncle! You may be from the sticks, but you ain't no hick. You don't talk like a hick." Her hand went up to Moe's face momentarily. "You are a sweet boy, Moe." She brushed her bangs aside and he saw her large brown eyes had grown misty.

A group of students were approaching obviously involved in spirited dialogue of one of the professor's lectures they'd just left. Moe and Alma Dean grew silent in their wake and waited until they passed before speaking again. They had begun walking toward Blossom Street, and gradually he became cognizant of the whine of the city bus and automobiles passing. Alma Dean had slowed her step. "I like it when the minutes take their time, don't you? Little minute, take your time. Little minute, take your time," she chanted.

He looked at her, uncertain of what to say, so he didn't say anything but walked on, reducing his own steps benevolently to match hers. After they'd walked a little longer, and he felt it adequate timing, he stopped, looked up into the sky and mumbled he'd better get back; he didn't want to miss supper; the dorm had rules.

Maybe the rest of the world wanted to reverse time, but time was only a vehicle to him and now it was traveling much too slowly. Where was Marty, and why was it taking so long for him to get well enough to come home?

"Will you come down to see us again? My sister and me'll teach you how to dance, and when you go back to wherever you're from, you can teach the girls there. You did like that new song by Kitty Wells, didn't you? You were dancing real good."

"I have many classes to study for. Papers, lectures, everyday."

"Well, it'ud do you good to get away onct in a while and

come dance. Now wouldn't it?"

"You don't understand. I—"

"You did like us, didn't you?

"That's not the point. I—"

"You have a girlfriend—you have a girlfriend, that's it!"

"No. No. I don't have a girlfriend. I've never had a girlfriend."

"Are you afraid of girls?"

"No. I don't have time for a girlfriend, that's all. I have my studies. I have friends, but I do not have a girlfriend."

Alma Dean looked at him incredulously.

"You see," he began, not wanting to tell her, someone he barely knew, about Marty and his being injured. And how could he explain his relationship with Marty anyway to someone like her. "I'm having a difficult time with trigonometry, you know. You see, in the school where I'm from we didn't have a teacher for trig and physics and chemistry and—"

"Wait a minute—"

"You probably have those courses here in these city schools, but we didn't. Our teachers were well educated and did the best they could do, but there were so few—"

"Wait a minute Moses-Moe. I wouldn't take any of those classes even if—"

"I'm sure you would if you wanted to. I understand the Pythagorean theorem; the square of the hypotenuse is the sum of the squares of the other two sides. C square equals A square plus B square, I understand that, but—"

"Huh?"

"But I didn't even have a slide rule before I got here. I'd never even heard of Euclid and—"

"Moe, you do need to come down and let Christine and me teach you to dance. All this college work is getting to you."

"No. I must study to make up for everything I missed in high school. But maybe I'll walk down again sometimes, but I can't say when."

Chapter Seventeen

Make money, money by fair means if you can,
if not, but any means money.

Horace

"You. Bazookaman Price," said Captain Cecilia Seabrook, Army nurse of 820 Mobile Surgical team.

From his bed, Marty looked not too high up. In fact, he saw that she was short and slightly out of focus but slightly familiar. "You're being moved today, Pvt. Price. Do you know where you are?" She checked and adjusted tubes and monitors.

Since that day he arrived, she was there. And everyday, she had said the same thing, asked the same questions. She seemed to search his eyes as if she expecting an answer. Today something in her voice demanded his eyes to focus. He strained as hard as he could. He had heard the part about being moved. He was going to be moved? He was losing her as a whisper reminded him he was not dead? What was she, this illusionary presence saying what he needed to hear?

"You've going to the Medical Aid Station in Yangzi, Pvt. Price. And you know what? My friend. We have bonded here, you and I, and I will miss you. You are breaking my heart. You have ignored me day after day, no matter how many times I have poured out my heart to you, you little cutie. I have fallen in love with you, but do you care? No, you just lie there ignoring me—rejecting the notion to get better and refusing to open your eyes and talk to me."

Something flickered and stopped Capt. Seabrook in her daily rambling dialogue. "Are you focusing? What—?"

She stared and bent swiftly. Was there a moment of recognition, or was she imagining? Did he actually try to speak?

"Pvt. Price, do you read me? Come in. Is there a person behind that handsome face?"

"Did you say *moving*?"

Suddenly, Capt. Seabrook's face broke into a smile as she lifted her head involuntarily toward the ceiling. "Yahoo!" she screamed. Patients, doctors, and other nurses turned to see the exultation on the face of a nurse who had devoted days and weeks to this coma-stricken private.

Marty blinked, trying to obliterate the faces of pain and the cacophony of clanks, hums, machines of swallowing death. Her face. He wanted it to stay in focus, but it would take fortitude to keep it from fading into nothingness again. He remembered it from a moment somewhere, bringing pain and then forcing him to endure it until he could not any longer.

"PFC Martin Price. Company C, 72nd Tank Battalion, Second US Infantry Division. Is that you, soldier? Answer affirmative if you are," she yelled.

He made an attempt to salute. "Yes, sir—ma'am," he managed. And tears came to the eyes of Capt. Seabrook.

Later, she returned to his bedside with a paper dish covered with a paper napkin. "Pvt. Price, guess what I've managed to smuggle in for you. Strawberries."

Marty gagged and threw up the first solid food he'd eaten for months.

Chapter Eighteen

There's no money in poetry, but then there's
no poetry in money, either.
Robert Graves

Saturdays were usually catch-up days, studying and writing the endless essays for class and reaching to grasp the difficult science and mathematical courses. His mother was never daunted in the least if he mentioned the level of difficulty of the college work. She smiled smugly, "You come from good stock on both sides. Your ancestors accomplished greatness, and you shall too." But today, he decided to leave off studying for a while. His feet felt sure and steady on the marble steps of McKissick Library, a fairly new building with domed Greek revival style with six columns. He began to walk back across the horseshoe. Moe had been told that the first president of the University of South Carolina in 1807 had lived in a house on this site. Some of the professors still talked about the "recent passing of the beloved President J. Rion McKissick even though he'd been dead since 1944. He looked at his wristwatch, 2:30. Too much afternoon left to go back to his dormitory just yet. He turned his steps toward the din of the city. He crossed Pendleton. He noticed that the leaves were beginning to fall already when the wind blew, and it had been blowing aggressively for several hours. He slowed his steps as he came upon Sumter Street.

There stood Trinity Episcopal Church and cemetery. Yes, and here were the tombs of some of his mother's relatives he'd heard her mention only rarely and secretively. He looked at the headstones encased in brick and wrought iron dignity. These people had belonged to a political system that built up and sustained and nourished this state. Yet something had happened before Moe's birth that caused the rift that divided the family. His maternal grandfather and his own father had never been able to get along. But it must have been more than that. His mother's people made her choose.

They'd more or less kicked her out of the family, excommunicated her from the society she'd grown up in. Why? What had happened? His mother never let an innuendo slip, and there was no one else who would know. Hannah, as long as she had been with the family, was not privy to that knowledge. And if so, she'd probably become too old to remember. It never occurred to him to ask about family matters. He had accepted it as one of the norms of life just as he had accepted his mother's eccentricities. He had grown to know she was unlike any other Britton's Neck mother, but he'd attributed that to his sister's disappearance and his father's death. But now he pondered that maybe his mother had more reason to be less than conventional. Maybe she and his father had come from a family of lunatics. He'd seen his father's ancestors' tombstones in the churchyard in Georgetown: William Henry Lackey, 1810-1857; William Wesley Lackey, 1842-1863; Davis Moses Lackey, 1860-1919, his grandfather. His own father now rested with them, Davis Moses Lackey, Jr., 1903-1942.

Before this moment, he'd never seen where his mother's family had claimed some expensive real estate in this Columbia cemetery in the heart of the capital city. Looking at the tombstones, he recognized some of the names from envelopes exchanged over the years and newspaper clippings his mother had cut out of *The State* and *The Post and Courier* newspapers. An eerie feeling crept over him as he realized quite a few of the people on the other side of the soil where he stood were actually the bodies that had produced him, yet he knew absolutely nothing about them. He'd never seen their faces or heard their voices because they had rejected his mother. Why—because she chose to marry his father, a Lackey from the lowcountry? It couldn't have been for lack of money. Wasn't his father as wealthy or wealthier than his mother? Moe had always taken for granted that both of them had descended from aristocratic families. They never had to work like other people. His father just seemed to run the mansion and property while his mother fidgeted with whatever notions she had on her mind at the current time.

He'd taken all of his life for granted really. Never looking at his life from the perspective of anyone other than Marty. He imagined Marty thought he was stuffy, smart, sensible, calculating, controlling, and owned by his mother. That's exactly how he thought of himself, and Marty was exactly the polar opposite.

Suddenly, Moe realized he was hungry. He gazed one last time at the number of graves bearing his mother's last name. Strange. He would need to investigate more deeply into this matter at some point in time. He may never know the cause of the chasm that had ripped his mother from her family, these prominent people, or why his parents had decided to settle on a plantation house in Britton's Neck of all places. Was it to be in such an isolated place that the two families could not or would not interfere in the relationship they had with one another? He may never know. He knew this though—he would never stoop to call on his mother's family no matter how powerful they were or how serious his trouble. He turned and began his walk back toward campus. He looked at his watch. He knew he'd miss the cafeteria unless he hurried. He must shove the complexities of his family history back into the crevices of his brain until a more convenient time.

He bent to pass beneath the low growing branches of the live oak tree cattycornering the McCutchen House gardens. A squirrel skittered across his path, momentarily startling him. After laughing at himself, he practically ran across the horseshoe toward Pinckney House. He was almost there when a shadow behind a huge mountain laurel lurched for him. Was it a ghost of an earlier ancestor? He tried to keep his pace constant.

"Hey!"

"Who is it?" He half asked, half demanded. Alma Dean, looking down, stood with the left hand covering most of her face.

"Alma Dean, I told you not to come back on campus. I—"

"I couldn't help it. I just had to see you."

He could tell now why she tried to shield her face. A bruise darkened her left eye and cheek. "What happened to your face? Were you injured?"

"Injured? Ha. Injured? Let's walk away from here. I don't

want any of your pals to see you talking to me."

They walked toward Maxey Gregg Park in an area where contractors had just begun a gigantic building project, Hendley Homes Apartments, for the growing student population of the university. Land had been cleared and foundations were being marked off and poured. Now it looked like the pale and red spots where scabs had been torn off an old sore. They walked to a grove in the park, and suddenly Alma Dean scooped her flared skirt close to her and flopped on the bare ground. Moe stood over her until she, looking at him pitifully, said, "Sit down."

Somehow he knew the conversation would be like many he'd had with his mother. He'd be drawn into the arena until she had said all she wanted to say, and it would be something he'd rather not hear, but he wasn't accustomed or equipped to stopping the talk. He also wasn't accustomed to talking one to one with girls. He felt a certain ambivalence shrouding this conversation. Her eyes and creamy complexion were her best features, and now they were tarnished. He closed his eyes. He must seem a total fool to her.

"Someone hit you, didn't they?" She nodded. "Who? Why?"

"You ain't the only man in the world, you know. There're more boys than you. I just can't help it that something about you draws me like a rat to cheese."

"Me?"

"Oh, I know I ain't nothing to you... you, a college boy... gonna be somebody... gonna graduate from college one day and be gone... I'll never see you again... you'll never think of me again... not once. Huh? Like as if you think of me now. Ha.

Why did you ever have to walk to Olympia anyways? My life's been pure hell since that day."

"Alma Dean, I never gave you any impression— I never—"

"I know you didn't. You ain't like no boy I ever seen. People think mill girls are kinda fresh, and here you come along... never danced... never drunk nothing... never lied to a girl to take advantage. The one person who don't want to take advantage takes all the advantage."

"Wait a cock-eyed minute. That's not fair. I'm sorry if that has happened."

Something in her outpouring emotional attraction to him stirred something in him. Pity? Compassion like he may feel toward a pet dog or a neighborhood animal that had been mistreated? He reached over to inspect the bruise. Fairly new. Not yet yellowing. She grabbed his hand with both of hers and pulled them to her lips, kissing his fingers, fingertips, palms. He could not draw himself away from her, yet he could not respond with equal ardor, feigned or real. She held his hand to the bruised area of her face and hoarsely spoke, "This is because of you. I tried to come see you, but he caught me and made me go back. I don't care about him. It's you I want to see. I don't care if he kills me. I'm with you now." She lay back, pulling him down almost on top of her. She began touching his body, making him feel awkward and excited, reckless, at the same time.

She had pulled him down partially pinning her thigh down, and he scrambled to remove his weight from her. She still held both his hands making him insecure in his position. Her eyes now took on a crazed look and searched his, seemingly unconscious of his precarious physical position. He had to jerk his right hand free to prevent his falling full force onto her face and upper body. His palm landed on a pinecone that tore his hand painfully, but he dared not complain as she was clearly in some kind of ecstasy. Her large hands reached up to pull his head down to her face. This could not be happening; his senses were guarded. He tried to survey the premises as his head was going downward to see if Alma Dean's tryst was a spectacle for passersby, as he could imagine it was. She did not seem aware that they were on public property in a semi-wooded area within a shouting distance of possibly hundreds of people. The lower branches of the pine thicket indeed made a kind of room blocking them from onlookers. Breathing was painful, and she was tearing at his shirt.

His thoughts were jumbled. Racing through his mind were bits and pieces of his recent days—Marty who may be wounded beyond recognition, his mother and her family's graves in the cemetery. For an instant he saw the graves opening and dead people jumping up like jack-in-the-boxes. "Dead!" they screamed. "We are dead and soon you'll be!" Here lay a willing girl although he never desired her and knew he never would and would never wish to see her again after today and would even make employment of dodging her for the rest of his life. He struggled. He fumbled. He moaned. Her eagerness excused his miscalculations. Then it was over, and his face lay on the pine straw carpet, and he wished he could disappear into and beneath it and not have to look at her or himself again. She was still panting and lying on her back on the pine straw, but she'd pulled her skirt back over her bare legs. He could smell the earth and the straw. His palm had blood on it. He closed his eyes to seal the deed he'd done.

The call came the next week. At last Marty was coming home. He would be arriving at Fort Jackson in Columbia.

PART TWO

Chapter Nineteen

I have enough money to last me the rest
of my life, unless I buy something.
Jackie Mason

Everyone, especially Marty, knew it wouldn't be long now. The morphine Moe was giving Polly was having little or no effect. Blanche, now widowed and retired, was there by her bedside, swabbing her face, making sure she was turned frequently to prevent any more of the horrible maggots that come from bedsores. He had limped into the room to see Blanche dousing his mother's back with whiskey and then turn up the bottle to douse her own sickness of weariness or maybe it was sorrow and disappointment in life. She'd discovered that life passes quickly and skips over the dreams people set out to achieve.

Somehow even in the omniscience of death a person can expect the end but not allow his mind to feel it. Marty tried to hold inside his hatred of Moe at the moment for not being able to revive Polly and all the other things that that had turned out badly in his life. All Moe could do was placate the pain; the erosion of Polly's cancer continued. Finally, he avoided any encounter with Moe. Once in awhile, his mind floated back to a memory of another redhead, Capt. Seabrook. Ironically, his time of severest pain brought the sweetest memory of his entire life. It was an oasis from the hell of his life.

"Marty, your mother is calling for you," Blanche said, her voice animated. "Come quickly."

He tried to organize his thoughts and emotions as he carefully laid down the wrenches on the hood of the Corvair he was working on for Coach Hendricks' wife. He placed them methodically on a wipe rag and then took another rag for his hands. Deliberately, he measured his stride, taking as careful and as long a step as possible with his slight limp across the yard and into the house and into the hall and into her room and then beside her bed where she looked dazed but deeply into his eyes.

"Marty, how are you? Are you okay?" Her voice was low from weakness. "My boy. My own Marty. The only good thing… the only thing to come out of my life."

He reached and took her hand—once strong enough to break a chicken's neck with one swift twist. Now, the fingers were nothing but yellowed skin over bones. Her hands were clammy, and her once crimson hair, now mostly white, was subdued on her neck and shoulders. She tried to lift her head, but he awkwardly touched her shoulders and hoarsely, said, "Don't try to sit up, Ma. Rest. Lay back and rest."

"There's something I need to tell you, Marty. It's important. Do you hear me?" Her voice sounded as if it would give out before she could say what she was determined to say. "It's about your daddy."

It was not that he'd never wondered about it—if the truth were known, about half his growing up years had been filled with illusions about his biological father. Many times he'd imagined his father had died like Moe's dad. In the past decade, it hadn't mattered so much, and now when he was about to lose his mother, it was like a fall on gravel tearing off the scab of an old wound, the smarting of the old faithful throb was there in his face, fresher and more painful than ever at this moment.

"You don't have to do this, Ma." He heard himself say, but in such ambiguity he couldn't believe it was his voice he was hearing.

"There was a highway patrolman down here working the... " her voice trailed off. She was too weak to go on. He waited while his mind raced. "He worked the chain gang... his name was... "

His mind was reeling like a gyroscope.

"He was an officer with the sheriff's office." Her head came off the pillow, and she searched his eyes. What did she hope to discover in his eyes—forgiveness, joy, acceptance? And the wait for the name, *the name*, was getting to be unbearable.

"He never knew you was even coming. I didn't know him but two weeks. And then he was gone, and you were on the way."

"Ma." All the questions of his childhood had dissipated in the air.

"Alvin Dozier was his name. He lived in Marion, I 'speck. I never went looking for him, nor him me. What was done was done." Her head fell back, and she was through with the story, the confession of her life. She wasn't dead, but now she could die.

Every word was emblazoned indelibly on his mind, burning, burning, *burning*. Marty tried to hide the fire just like he had all his life. Her eyes were closed, and her mouth tight—there would be no more on the subject. He began fumbling with the top sheet to feign making her comfortable. After an eternity of a moment, he stumbled out of the room, avoiding Blanche's eyes for he knew Aunt Blanche was searching desperately to read him and his emotions. Three days later, Pauline Price was dead.

Sleep had for the past two decades been a luxury ill afforded to Marty. He came close to asking Moe for sleeping pills but knew deep down, he would fall in love with pills, and they would mean his death. He had survived all the pain of his wounds; he would survive now. Alvin Dozier shouldn't be too hard to find. The name loomed before him as he tried to sleep during the night and as he strove to be awake during the day. He was waiting until the dirt had been thrown over the casket where Polly now lay beside her maw, paw, and his uncle Harold. There was a plot remaining for Aunt Blanche. His mama was finally at a home she could be proud of at last. Old Neck Cemetery was a community that made all the residents equal.

As in all other matters in his life, Marty wasn't going to share this new vendetta with anyone. He knew his aunt Blanche could help if he asked her for information because she knew everyone in the county and the six surrounding counties, plus, she had lived through it and might even have more information on the subject. But he had all the information he needed—the name, Alvin Dozier—the son of a bitch. Besides, Aunt Blanche might try to convince him not to do what he knew he wanted to do more than anything else in the world. She had found Jesus and was at Mt. Nebo Baptist Church every time the doors opened and couldn't seem to do enough good around the community. He didn't have anything against it. He just didn't want to get into that. Korea had been his battle; this was his war.

Chapter Twenty

I don't care too much for money
for money can't buy me love.
John Lennon and Paul McCartney

Marty circled the block several times before he zeroed in on parking his white '63 Impala with its red interior—his favorite car of all time—one he'd bought brand new and kept it looking like the day he drove it off the lot. His eccentricities included parking his car so that no idiot (his words) would open a door into it. But that wasn't the reason he hovered before stopping. He had been confused by the information that Alvin Dozier was a patient in a nursing home. He didn't want any new emotion to come into play in his fight. He wanted pure, raw hatred only. No matter how hard he tried not to, his limp always made people stare. *DAMNYOU people*, he always thought when he saw people openly staring at him.

The nursing home was not the best one in the area by a long shot. On the outskirts of Marion, it was a one story with a low roof and a ton of roll out windows. The sidewalk was cracked in a thousand different places, and the acorns from the nearby oak trees crunched beneath his feet as he made his way to the couple of steps with the rusty wrought iron railing. A stench met his nostrils as soon as he walked through the door. He stood in front of an empty desk for several moments looking down one hall and then the other. Here and there he saw old people bent over in wheel chairs looking as if they had been placed near a window and forgotten. Was one of these people Alvin Dozier? How would he know? Would he resemble him in some way? Would he be short like Marty? A characteristic Marty hated. Would he have piercing black eyes and wide teeth?

A middle-aged woman with a gray sweater carelessly worn walked up to the desk finally. "Morning. Can I help you?"

Marty worked his mouth robotically. He had never said out loud the man's name. He wanted to sound normal when he said it. "I want to see Alvin Dozier. Mr. Alvin Dozier."

"I don't remember seeing you here before. How long since you've seen him? He gets worser every day, you know," she rambled without stopping, and Marty was glad, for he didn't have to supply answers to her questions. "He's in the room at the end of the hall on the left."

Marty noticed the rooms didn't have numbers or names on them and that each room looked the same—small with a dingy little bed. A single little night stand with a lamp and picture. Some rooms had a few little forgotten looking flowers in pots in the window. Marty built up his steel as he got closer. He was going to openly confront him and make the announcement, "Hey you sonofabitch, I'm the bastard you left behind in Britton's Neck back in 1933. Want to see what a good job you did?" He stopped before he took the final step that would put him in the doorway of the last room on the left. He heard a voice, a man's voice, speaking in a low, monotonous tone. He stood there for a minute eavesdropping. The voice was too low to be audible. Marty turned and walked back to the desk.

"He's got somebody in there with him. I'll come back later."

"Oh, that's just his son." She looked back down at the paperwork she was doing.

Marty went to his car. A son. A legitimate son. His chest hurt. Probably the pride of his life. Probably rich, and smart, with lots of friends and lots of land here in Marion. Probably a nice, big house with some of these oak trees on the lawn. Probably a nice mother who belongs to a bridge club. Probably never suspected one damn minute his old man would have another kid off somewhere in the sticks. He was too angry now to try to break the news to him today. He drove around town for a while before turning the Impala toward the twenty-mile drive back to Britton's Neck.

After a couple days, Marty could stand the build up of hate no longer. He had finished checking the Hendrickses' Corvair. It was a beauty of a car, and these two, who had been teaching at Britton's Neck since he had been a student, were the type who loved anything that looked expensive. The Corvair was different all right with the motor in the back. The front was similar to his baby, but the Impala was sporty with the tail fins and sleek lines. They'd paid $600 for the Corvair, same as he'd paid for the Impala, but now they wanted to make sure they had gotten a good deal. Or so they said. He often thought they were checking up on him and Moe more than anything. He gave them a call and said the car was ready and they could leave the money under the brick.

This time he went directly to the nursing home and

bypassed the lady at the desk. She, however, wasn't going to let him get by so easily this time. She must have been asking around about him. "Young man. I 'speck you're going to see Mr. Dozier again today. Um? Who did you say you were?"

"I didn't say, ma'am. But I'm Marty Price coming to visit Mr. Dozier."

"I told his son 'bout you coming by the other day, and he couldn't figure out who you were. Don't many people come to see Mr. Dozier."

"Is that right? Why you think that is?"

"Well, he ain't got no body but his son. And his son, bless his heart, he does the best he can, I reckon, but he can't come often to see his poor old daddy. His daddy has dementia. Why, he don't even know his own son most of the time, and it's getting worse every day. Can't remember if he's even eat his breakfast." She clucked her tongue and shook her head. "When Doug comes back, you want me to tell him you come by?"

"That's left up to you, ma'am." He walked toward the end of the hall, last room on the left. He still wanted Alvin Dozier to know he had another son, one who hated his guts. He stepped through the door and glared at the body on the smelly bed. Long legged, dried up, gaunt. His eyes were closed, and his mouth open as if in a perpetual yawn. He had tuffs of graying hair in gross disarray above his leathery face. Marty studied the form in front of him and knew this man would never comprehend the vileness he felt for him. Damn, another failed enterprise. He couldn't even avenge his mother. He couldn't get the revenge she deserved out of this piece of human crap lying here in this miserable bed.

But, Marty's eyes began to squint. But—he has a son. The sins of the father will be visited on the son. That sounded biblical as if God himself would allow him to be redeemed through the retaliation on the legitimate son, mister high and mighty son. Yes, God would not hold it against Marty if he took his vengeance out on the son. Even though Marty was not as strong as before Korea, he knew he could still be a power keg when he needed to be. He would beat this son to a pulp and leave his dying body in the Pee Dee River.

He didn't even hear the soft footsteps of the man walking into the room. Only out of the side of his eye did he get a glimpse of him as he walked around Marty still standing between the door and the bed. The man walked around Marty and to the other side of the bed, so that the old man's emaciated skeleton was between them.

"Hey. I'm Doug. I'm his son. I don't believe I ever met you."

"No. We haven't met before." Marty scanned the features and could have been looking at a version of himself. Doug was his height but thinner. Even with his former injuries, Marty looked in better shape than this man. He looked his same age, but he appeared timid to the point of being afraid.

"Miss Ellen, out there at the desk, called me and said you were back. I live right across the street. She didn't know who you were but thought I'd like to see you, if you are family, and all. Are you family? Sorry I don't remember you if you are. I never went to the family reunions. Hated them. Since Mama died, I've been on the road pretty much. That is, until they called me and said they had to do something with Daddy. He kept getting lost and couldn't remember his way home—even if it was just down the street. Caught him one time going in this black woman's house thinking it was his. He'd forgotten where he left the car. Couldn't tell anybody where he lived. The police all knew him for when he worked with them. They looked out for him for as long as they could. You can't blame them for what they did. They called my trucking company and told them to git me down here on the double; something had to be done and quick. I had no idea he was this bad. He don't even know me. He won't know you, probably."

Marty listened and for the first time in his life began to feel something in the universe was right by being wrong. The cadaverous body lying before these two young men had produced by two different women two men who were alike by more than genes. Their histories must be intertwined. He was feeling it more so than knowing it, and he needed to know more. Why? How can God make two men, who lived their lives twenty miles apart for forty years and never knew each other, be alike in bones and brains? He suddenly felt he was going to be sick. The emptiness of Polly's house since they'd buried her and the arsenal of hatred he had built up for a man that he would never be able to expend were causing his insides to feel they were turning inside out.

"I've got to get out of here."

"I don't know who you are coming here to see my daddy, and I don't know where you're from, but the least I can do is buy you a hamburger. Let me take you to the grill. They make the best hamburgers in Marion."

As they sat across the table at the Marion Grill, Doug couldn't stop talking. Marty let him talk. His own mind was still in limbo. He still hated his guts for being a legitimate son, but not so much as he did at first.

"My wife can't take my drinking. She can't take my being gone for weeks at a time when I have to do a run cross the country, which is every month. You know, it was President Ike that signed off on the Interstate Highway System, and since then trucking is the way of the future. I make pretty good at driving. And I'd make a ton more if I had my own rig, but I'm not set for that—not now, maybe in the future. She can't take the debt and living from paycheck to paycheck. I know she's slipping around, and it's just a matter of time before she leaves me for some better offer that comes along. Hell, I don't even care anymore. Don't you think that's strange? But I don't. I'm through with caring about a woman who don't love me. She's never once been in that home to see my daddy. I guess she's hanging around to see what she'll get out of it all when he kicks the bucket. Well, he ain't got pea-turkey squat, so there. That'll get the best of her.

"Ain't that the best hamburger you ever ate? I eat on the highway a lot, and there ain't no better in any state I been in. Hey, I'm doing all the talking. Are you ever going to tell me how we are related?"

Marty slowly chewed his hamburger and picked up two long French fries and stuck them in his mouth. He shook his head and looked at Doug. He had never had anyone but Moe as a friend. Never had anyone else except his mother, Aunt Blanche, and Uncle Howard. Here was someone who was a failure, just like he was. What would happen if he told him the truth? Would the truth make him a friend? Did he even want this loser for a friend? Two losers do not a good relationship make. Or did it? Would the truth make Doug hate him as much as he had started out hating Doug? Would he be surprised to know that twenty miles away from here there had been another world that his father had ruined?

"Let me tell you a story," Marty began.

Chapter Twenty-One

If you can count your money,
you don't have a billion dollars.

J. Paul Getty

As the years had come and gone, Violet had become more and more reclusive. Hannah had finally withered away. Her only help was the wine she drank around the clock. One day Violet locked herself in her room and refused to come out. She was sixty-six. When he forced open the door, to his horror, Moe found the sanctuary she'd built to Hazeline. Candles were burning dangerously throughout her room. She had become disheveled and filthy. The stench was unbearable. His first reaction was to try to act with no reaction. Let your professionalism take over, he told himself. She looked at him as if he were a stranger.

"Mother, can you hear me?" he asked dubiously.

"Who are you?" she looked and spoke timorously.

"Mrs. Violet, can you hear me?" he asked again. "This is your doctor. Can you tell me where you are?"

"Hello, Doctor. I'm Mrs. Davis Lackey. My son is a doctor also. Have you ever met him? We had a daughter—Hazeline. I can't remember where she went. Did you ever meet her? Have you seen her recently?"

"No, Mrs. Lackey. But I think we'd better arrange for you

to go to a place where you might be able to talk to some other folks. Would you like that?"

"Oh, I'm not sure I can leave this place. You see, this is the place Hazeline will come back to one day. If I leave, she will not be able to find me."

"I tell you what, Mrs. Lackey, I'll let your son know where you are going. Then if your daughter comes back, he can take her to you. How does that sound?"

"I still don't think I can leave here. I don't have permission to leave. You see, my husband, Mr. Lackey, said I cannot leave for a long, long time. I don't think he would like it if I were to leave."

"Why is that, Mrs. Lackey? Why don't you have his permission to leave?"

Violet's right hand went up to her forehead and she turned her face and body from side to side, as if she were a little girl trying to make a very difficult decision. She squirmed and turned her head in such growing agony, Moe spoke softly, "It's all right, Mrs. Violet. You can tell me later if you like."

"I think I'd better wait till later. I need a sip of something sweet, if you don't mind, Doctor."

"You've probably had too much of this right now. Let me get you some water and get you to the bathroom and perhaps into a shower. How does that sound?"

"I need something to drink," she said with urgency.

"Well, just one last little drink while I call a nurse."

Moe needed help, and he knew he had made a significant discovery to learning what had happened in the past. He went to the phone and called the Hendrickses. They were on the way.

The older teacher, Mrs. Hendricks, and the younger Mrs. Rogers had formed a reciprocal relationship that had matured as they had. Mrs. Rogers' husband, turned down by the military, had returned to teaching. Coach Hendricks had retired, but his wife still taught, hanging on to the title as teacher who had been in the district the longest. The foursome was usually seen together wherever they went, and recently they frequented antique car shows. The Hendrickses no longer lived in the teacherage apartment but had bought a modest house closer to Marion. Coach Hendricks, as he was still known, was often dropping off photographs and plans at Dr. Lackey's and dropping off cars at Marty's for Marty to pass inspection on. Coach Hendricks also had become more of a regular at the old Lackey home, offering his services in any way he could. He had been the school's former science teacher, and granted, the curricula didn't offer an extensive range when he taught, Coach Hendricks still had the knowledge of some scientific matters in common with Moe. Gradually, he had taken to overseeing the books for the doctor.

It was more a matter of convenience that Moe accepted the offers of help from Coach Hendricks. Then Mrs. Hendricks somehow got in the picture though he couldn't tell how. To Moe, the Hendrickses' constant generosity was overwhelming at times. It had been highly unlike any other times in his life; no one had ever gone overboard giving him attention. Occasionally, their unmerited favor reminded him of Alma Dean and made him shutter to think of the hurt of that long ago experience. Sometimes he'd shake his head thinking how absurd he was becoming in his middle age. The mansion, which had always been somewhat of a mausoleum, became more of a tomb these days unless the Hendrickses and at times Mrs. Rogers happened to pop in, which was more and more often. It was common knowledge that Moe had always been isolated socially except for Marty, but Marty hadn't been by the mansion for months. His last visit left a door to the end open.

The last time Marty had come by for an evening, he told Moe about finding his real father and half brother named Doug. Marty had never talked about his father, but he had wanted to go into detail about him and Doug, but for some reason, Moe could feel himself clamming up, becoming cold and distant. Marty had begun to see more and more of Doug and less of Moe. It had been a strain on everyone since Polly's cancer took her life. Moe's own mother Violet was withdrawing more and more into her old shell and becoming noticeably incoherent.

Marty had never been one for visiting the mansion often. Moe went to Marty's place. Moe had practically lived around the bay at the cinder block auto shop under the wide-spread branches of the live oaks with their dangling moss during their teen years, and then when Marty returned from the war, broken and bitter, Moe was there every time he came home from the university. By the time Moe was in medical school, Marty had improved physically to the point he could drive and several times visited Moe in Charleston. He had been suffering emotionally, but Moe had given him space and listened, and even if there was no dialogue between them for hours, they both understood each other back then, and Moe stuck by him.

When Marty did stop by the mansion, he often found

Coach Hendricks there, lurking and spying, he thought. When he asked about Mrs. Violet, he was told that she was in her room. He found it best to avoid going to the mansion altogether. Besides, after learning of Doug's existence and seeing how Doug responded favorably to having a brother, albeit, illegitimate, he felt a newness of spirit that he could not explain exactly. Doug had discussed with Marty his plans to get a divorce to which Marty yelled, "Hallelujah! Don't put it off one more damn minute. Be a man!" To Marty's surprise, Doug saw a lawyer the next day and began proceedings. Their drinking had produced a bonding of sorts; they could drink till midnight and still not be drunk. They felt their best decisions were made while partaking, imbibing of the fruit of the vine or corn or rye or whatever. Their friendship had become a more or less freer time for Marty again. He forgot he was limping. He sometimes found himself laughing from his gut. He didn't have to answer to anyone. He avoided going to the cemetery after his mother died, but now he felt better if he took a few minutes every now and then to just ride to Old Neck and walk around her grave and once in a while put a little flower he'd picked from Aunt Blanche's yard on top of the headstone.

He did have tinges of guilt occasionally about not stopping more often to see Aunt Blanche. Over the past few years of watching Polly grow sicker and sicker, Blanche had grown in grace more than anyone he'd ever known. Most likely when he stopped by, she would be sitting in her little living room beside the lamp reading the Bible along with her Sunday School book. Usually she had a stack of get well or happy birthday cards on the table, so she could write messages and mail to members of the church and community.

As inseparable as they used to be, it was hard to believe Marty rarely visited or saw Moe any longer. He hadn't meant to stop by the mansion, but one dark night it was getting late, and he saw the ambulance and the Corvair parked in the driveway in front of the mansion. It didn't take but a few minutes to see that it was indeed Mrs. Violet who was the patient. Moe was walking beside the gurney, which the EMTs were pushing to the waiting vehicle.

When she saw Marty, she motioned for them to stop. She looked up at him intently. She reached for his hand and said, "Polly, I told you we'd get your boy home. Now if we can only get Hazeline back. If—they will only give her back."

The ambulance pulled off and the Hendrickses said they'd follow it to Marion Memorial Hospital. Moe said he'd check on her in the early morning before he opened the office. Marty didn't know why but his mind soured on the idea that the Hendrickses were getting so thickly associated with Moe Lackey. What was their angle, he wondered. They'd never been friends with anyone from the Neck. His own mother Polly, who never discussed her personal life, had alluded to their ill treatment of her at school, never once saying as much as a "good morning" or "thank you."

A week later Marty, after hearing about Mrs. Violet's being sent to a Georgetown nursing home for special treatment, wanted to verify all he'd heard. "Oh, look who's here. It's Marty Price," said Mrs. Hendricks, coming to the door as if she owned the place. She was holding her drink in her chubby hand and laughing with her head slightly back. "Come on in, Mr. Price. We're just back in the den finishing a game of cards."

Marty began to follow her back to the den past the curio that had always stood in the foyer. As a child he'd felt terror in coming into such a big house with all the museum-like furniture and other finery. He's made a ritual of looking at a Chinese porcelain plate, red with gold flowers around the rim, on a stand in the curio when he passed. The plate had a court lady in the center playing with two little boys beside a bridge. He had always imagined the boys were he and Moe, and the lady was protecting them or warning them to be careful if they went over the bridge. He immediately noticed it was not there. When he was little, the court lady warded off evil spirits and kept him safe. Now, he felt a tremor in his bones—perhaps it was the evil spirit in the mansion. Surely he was imagining things.

Marty quickly saw the foursome around the table, Moe appearing to be more than slightly inebriated. He looked up at Marty and then held up his card hand. "You just might bring me luck. I need it playing with these card sharks. Come on in."

"When did you take up gambling—to add to your other vices?" Marty's voice was surlier than he expected it to be.

"He's not doing too bad for a beginner. Tonight he was doing okay for awhile." Coach Hendricks seemed to be trying to balance the scene.

"Well, it looks to me like he's had enough of this and needs to call it quits. What you say, Moe?"

"Nah. My friends here... " he mumbled and then tried to focus on Marty, but his eyes didn't work well.

Mrs. Rogers was already stacking up her cards as if she knew the game was over.

Marty looked from face to face, "I'd say the game has been going on too long already. Come on, Moe, put your cards on the table."

Mrs. Hendricks began to gather up the glasses and booze and cart them off to the kitchen. Mr. Hendricks swooped up the stack of cash on the table. "Well, I did win fair and square. Maybe you'll do better next time. I guess we had better get out of here since Dr. Lackey's friend is here."

Marty was growing more and more confident that they were taking advantage of Moe. His anger was mounting fast, and they sensed it. "It will be our bedtime when we get back to Marion," Coach Hendricks said, his eyes narrow slits in the upper part of his face just before the large bald forehead began. He had once had a stock of yellowish hair; now it was a mix of blond and gray and his tanned cap line was the only division between face and head. He had once been physically fit, but now he was the product of too much booze and too much time and not enough exercise. His wife, on the other hand, although her blond hair had grayed around her face and her body had rounded out, appeared more energetic than ever. He didn't know Mrs. Rogers; she was not around when he was in school, but immediately he could tell she was a mousy disciple of Mrs. Hendricks.

After they'd made their quick departure, Marty sat across from Moe. "How much did you lose?"

"Aw, I dun know. I'm not so good as I used to be."

"You're freaking drunk! That's why. What's come over you? You're letting these people in your house and letting them take over. Damn! No use talking to a drunk. You won't know a thing I've said in the morning. I came by to ask about Mrs.

Violet, but you're not in any shape to talk about her either."

"Marty, she's gone. Mother is gone off in the head," Moe whined in his drunken stupor.

Marty helped him get up the stairs to his room. "You better get your head on straight and soon. Them people are going to take you to the cleaners."

The following day Marty noticed the doctor's office was closed, but it was often closed on Saturday nowadays. Dr. Lackey's office had been a commodity in Britton's Neck for almost two decades. People had thought a clinic would follow his coming back to doctor the community, but no clinic had come. People still had to go to Conway, Marion, or Florence to a hospital. When his mother had been his receptionist and bookkeeper; she dunned people to death until they paid their bills. Since she'd gotten too nervous to work, a variety of other young women had been employed to do the jobs of bookkeeper and nurse. Dr. Lackey had no idea the status of the books. He assumed the books were in order.

Marty turned into the driveway where he'd been the night before and then went inside. Hannah used to be there each time he came, and in her slow pace would automatically fix his breakfast along with Moe's. He couldn't remember exactly how or when Hannah was no longer there, but it had been awhile. He called and then went on through the house to the kitchen and put on coffee, making it stronger than usual. "Moe, come on down here and face the music," he called as loudly as he could.

Ten minutes later he ascended the winding stairs and beat on Moe's door, then went inside and shook the covers until Moe turned face up and farted. His hair, which was beginning to gray around the ears and thin on top, was disheveled. His bed looked as if he hadn't moved the entire night. His mouth looked dry and smelt like a fish factory. Marty finally managed to get him to fumble down the stairs.

"And what do I owe this honor? Having you back? Oh, coffee. I think I need it."

"You need more than coffee. You need your head examined. You're a mess, a damn mess. Worse off than any patient you have."

"Shut up. Please." Moe hung his head as he drank another cup of coffee.

Marty leaned back in his chair, surveying the situation. Moe had been there for Marty when Marty returned from Korea in the mess he was in. Moe sometimes had lied to Violet and not returned to attend classes when he said he was so that he could be there for Marty through the long, dark nights. It had been a crawl for Marty. Now Marty felt it was his turn to step in to help Moe—if too much time had not been lost.

"Moe, how much are the Hendrickses doing to 'help' you?"

"What do you mean? I'd be lost right now without their help. Mother started to get . . . er . . . sick. They were—" It was still too early in the day for Moe to analyze or relate.

"When—how did the Coach and his fat wife worm their way in here?"

"Martin. What are you getting at?"

"How much did you lose last night? And the night before? And the night before that? And another thing, what happened to the China plate in the hallway?"

"What are you talking about? China plate? First one thing and then another. Slow down. What in the world do you think you're doing, coming in here accusing, and asking about—and now—what about the China plate?"

"There used to be a plate in the cabinet in the hallway. I don't know about such things, but I just imagine it was worth a pretty penny. The one with the two boys and the court lady and the gold flowers. Have you noticed it is gone? Did you sell it? Did you give it away? I am just wondering, Moe. Come here and I'll show you." Moe stumbled behind him to the hall and the curio. "There used to be—as long as I can remember—a Chinese plate sitting right there. Now where is it?"

Moe was silent.

"Now. When you have time. You better start to think about what's going on here. Mrs. Hendricks used to bully Ma around like she was some kind of god and Ma was trash. Ma always told me to watch out for her and don't make her mad. I just don't trust them, coming in here 'helping you out.' What else have they done for you?"

"Look here, Marty. I can appreciate all your good will, but where have you been lately, huh? You found out you have a half brother, and you spend every minute of your time with him. What am I to you, huh? We used to be buddies—but damn. I don't want to be having this conversation with you. It's really none of your business now, is it?"

"All right, I'll leave you alone. But, if I were you, I'd keep my eyes open when they're around. If I were you, I'd look after my own finances too and—"

"But you're not me. You sound like a jealous teenager."

"That does it, Moe Lackey. Have it your way. But if you find you are out of every penny your folks ever left you, don't say I didn't warn you."

Chapter Twenty-Two

Money is the sinew of love as well as war.

Dr. Thomas Fuller

Moe remained angry all morning. The mansion seemed bigger than ever. He almost never frequented any rooms except his bedroom, the kitchen, and the den. Now, with an aching head, he roamed the rooms. How would he know what belonged here and what was missing—if anything was missing. The nerve of Marty suggesting that items had been removed from the premises. Perhaps, he would take an inventory. Nothing of his mother's really had ever mattered to him before. Just things. What would happen to them anyway after she died? And then after *he* died? The rich relatives, that he didn't even know the names of, would descend on the mansion as if it were horse dung and air lift out anything of monetary value that had been passed down in the Lackey family. Nevertheless, the Chinese plate—what had happened to it? When was the last time he'd seen it? Did it get broken and Hannah disposed of it? No. If Marty had always noticed it, as he said, then he'd have noticed it while Hannah was alive.

As the afternoon wore on, he began to think of the recent proposition Coach Hendricks had made him. The investment. Coach had come across a sure way to invest some of the Lackey funds to increase his bank account before he decided to retire. He'd never been too much on finances. His mother had been the one who took care of the family money and had not discussed those matters with him. And lately she hadn't discussed much of anything with anybody. He had always been the obedient son and done what he was told. He would bring the matter up to Coach and ask about it. He would also take a look at the books. Probably wouldn't be able to make hide nor hair out of them, but just to be on the safe side, maybe he should. Besides, Marty had never said or done one thing that had hurt the Lackeys. Maybe he was growing jealous because of Moe's new friends. All the same, it would not hurt to be careful.

He was right; he couldn't make heads or tails out of the books. The nurse-receptionist possibly could help and he would plan to discuss it with her on Monday. Meanwhile he telephoned Coach Hendricks, but he wasn't in, according to Mrs. Hendricks. Was something the matter? Should they come down to Britton's Neck? No, he just wanted to ask about the office accounts and jot down some information about the investment scheme Coach had been working on. She'd have Coach call him later today or tomorrow, Sunday.

As soon as she hung up the phone, Mrs. Hendricks began to put two and two together. Marty Price was the cause of this call—Marty Price who had always been closer than a Siamese twin to Moe. They should have known he'd stick his nose into their plans sooner or later. Well, so be it. She knew just what would keep him quiet. She'd suspected all along since they'd been in high school that they were "different." They never had anything to do with anyone else; they hung together constantly. Now, it would be easy to get Moe to see how green eyed with jealousy Marty Price was that Moe had new friends. Yes, Marty was dying of jealousy because they were taking his friend away from him. It wouldn't be hard to convince anyone in Britton's Neck about that!

Sunday night and Marty and Doug had been drinking beer for about an hour at Doug's house as they watched a football game, something Marty had never been interested in since Britton's Neck only had basketball. The school had been too small to support an athletic program when he was a student. He was learning to appreciate many other things since his friendship with Doug. Doug had often asked him to go with him to the nursing home to visit their dad, but Marty didn't want to go that far just yet. Doug's divorce was settled, and he seemed to be progressing fairly well financially, if not entirely emotionally.

"You wanna hear a weird story?" Marty began. "My old pal, Moe—he's the doctor down in Britton's Neck—you remember him, don't you? Well, I have a reasonable suspicion that these two old teachers—heck, they live up here in Marion—the Hendrickses—do you know them? He used to coach, but he's retired. She's still teaching—must be a hundred years old and still teaching. Well, I have reasonable concern that they are swindling Moe."

"Hendrickses? I don't believe I ever heard of 'em, but I could find out quick enough." Doug reached for a pen and writing pad from a small table below the wall telephone. "What's his first name?"

"Coach."

"C-o-a-c-h. Wait a minute. That's his job; not his name."

"Let me see. All I ever called him was Coach. Maybe if I

saw it in the phone book, I'd recognize it. Can't be too many Hendrickses, can there?"

Doug retrieved a telephone directory after searching in several cabinets above the counter and below. The small twenty-page directory was in the miniscule drawer of the table below the wall phone.

"Here's three. Charlie, J.B., and Ken."

"Ken. Now I remember. We used to say Ken and his Hen. Her name is Henrietta. That's it, all right."

"Wait a minute. You say they are swindling the doctor? You got any proof? You're mighty little to be throwing such big claims around, ain't you?"

"Look, I know what I know. I can feel it in my gut. They are up to no good. Cheating the doctor at card games, and he ain't never played cards, and they're playing for stakes."

"Lord have mercy! We will expose the Ken and his Hen! Yes, we will. My daddy—our daddy—didn't work at the police department for all those years for nothing. All I have to do is call one of his old buddies to run a check on them. For once, we can do something right to help someone else! Can't we?"

The first of the week, Marty dropped by the school auto mechanics shop, as he was prone to do from time to time when his work was slow. They often could give him a day's work along and along—a motor they'd pulled that he could repair. Even with his war wounds, he was still the one that everyone recognized as the expert. They knew there had never been a motor he couldn't fix. He had never been a guy for making small talk, but he asked about the other teachers and listened closely when he mentioned the Hendrickses. He quickly detected that more was being conveyed from what the guys weren't saying. They immediately clammed up. He left feeling his visit had uncovered something, but he didn't know what. However, it didn't take long to find out.

Aunt Blanche wheeled into his yard, slammed on brakes, and was on her way to his door before he could button up his shirt. "Marty, we need to talk."

"Calm down, Aunt Blanche. Whatever it is, it can't be that bad."

"Yes, sir, it can be that bad. You know how Britton's Neck is! Talk travels faster than Southern Bell phone lines ever did. Do you know what's being said about you?"

"Me? No," he drawled, "and I don't care."

"Marty, Moe Lackey has found out that someone is embezzling from his accounts. Valuable antiques are being stolen from his home. And talk is that you are the only one who possibly could be guilty."

"Damn! They work fast." He blurted out as he turned, speaking to the opposite wall. Marty had never calculated that the Hendrickses would be smart enough to go this far. What a trick—blaming him for their little enterprise. Turning back to Blanche, he asked, "How do you know this? What's the talk?"

"You know how people here are— 'they said,' 'he said' — that kind of talk. Sooner or later, people begin to believe the most outrageous lies no matter what! I overheard someone at the store telling it."

"Well, you know it ain't—and couldn't possibly be so, don't you?"

"Of course! I know it but the damage is out there—on the tongues of people who don't really know how to discern truth from fantasy. But that doesn't keep these people from spreading malicious gossip. One more raging fire to hurt somebody—that's all the excitement some of these people want."

"Listen, Aunt Blanche. Ain't nobody gonna believe that I, Marty Price, stole one red cent from Moe Lackey. We been buddies since grammar school. Everybody knows that. Moe ain't gonna let nobody believe I ever took one little thing from him."

"You remember how sick you were when you came home from Korea? People saying you came back deranged in your mind." She turned her back and spoke lower. "They are saying since you are illegitimate, you are out to get revenge on Moe since he has turned on you. That you and he were – lovers."

Marty stood facing her back. He sighed as if all the wind in his lungs had escaped. An ugliness had come over him that pervaded his little room, his little world. Everything he had ever touched had turned bad and resulted in pain. His life, which was never meant to be and never should have been, had left a mark, a scar on everything he ever looked at. Perhaps that was the full portent of the strawberry birthmark—it meant that forever he would mar the lives of others just by association. And what had it left him? Nothing. Not one person in the entire world had ever really loved him for who he was—because he was nothing—not intended to be anything—not even intended to be *period*. What was life anyway but one pain after another? One joyless day after another. His years growing up with Moe Lackey, the rich boy who had everything he himself had not—the two of them drawn together by a common thread—not having the one thing that really matters, a daddy and a family. Their friendship was based on need. Would they even have been friends if they had had fathers?

Aunt Blanche turned and took his shoulders in her hands. "Marty, you are being framed. There's a Judas out there. I believe in you. You could never have done any of these things. I know you. I'm your aunt. I've seen you grow up. If you are closer than a friend with Moe—"

"But I'm not, Aunt Blanche! We are friends. We have been close friends, like brothers. I'm not sure what we are, but it's not sick and evil like you say people are saying!"

"I don't know what to do, but we are not going to let this get any more out of hand than it already has." She sucked in her breath, trying to disassociate the muddled issues in her head. She had to believe Marty about his relationship with Moe and leave it at that for the time being and go on to the criminal issue that was more pressing. "Marty, who could be embezzling from Dr. Lackey? Surely not his nurse; she's not that knowledgeable of a girl."

"Aunt Blanche, I know who's behind all this, but I can't go and tell everything I know without proof. I can't even tell you. You'll just have to believe me."

"Moe has family connections that—if they come in here and start turning over things—they can get to the bottom of this mess in a hurry. Although, they aren't as powerful as they used to be, and if they come in, it will be for the whole wide world to know and read about in the papers."

"But Moe is definitely not going to call on his mama's ritzy family, I can tell you that for sure. Doug and me are trying to find out some things on the sly."

"Doug Dozier? Oh, my little Marty," she said tearfully.

She had admitted to him after Polly's confession that she had known all along. She worked for the phone company; it would be hard not to know people in three counties. "I didn't know you two had gotten to be buddies. That might shed some light on things."

"I can't get into it with you right now. Like I said, we gotta have proof, and Doug is working on it. He drives a truck and knows lots of people."

Things were happening faster than he had counted on. His mind moved slowly in some ways. Doug called that same night to say he'd uncovered the fact that Coach was not above buying drugs. "Keep this under your hat, for now. We don't know who we can trust right now."

"I think it's time I pay another visit to Moe. My aunt came by and said the grapevine has it—get this—that I'm the one bamboozling Moe and that ain't all."

Doug's end of the line was silent.

"You hear me?" said Marty.

"Yeah. Don't take it personal. Okay?"

"That's easy for you to say. You the one who's legit."

Chapter Twenty-Three

Money can't buy friends, but you
can get a better class of enemy.
Spike Milligan

Marty could feel the icy reception but chose to ignore it. Moe's door had been locked, and he was forced to knock and wait before entering the mansion. "Well," Moe said and stood there.

"Let me in. We need to talk." Marty walked by brushing his shoulder. "I'm glad you are alone tonight. Let's have some coffee."

Moe followed him into the kitchen and sat down. Marty had a way of taking over sometimes. Marty waited until the coffee had made, poured two cups and sat down. If they'd been smokers, they'd have lit up, but they'd never gone that route. Marty noticed how shaky Moe's hand was as he reached for his cup. He'd seen men in Korea on dope. He looked at Moe's eyes to see that his pupils were dilated. *Amphetamines or some other drug*, he thought.

"Are you taking drugs?" Marty blurted out.

"Hell no. What's the matter with you?"

"Have the Hendrickses been here?"

"Why do you keep bringing them up? What have you got against them?"

"Listen, Moe. Your eyes are popping. Your hands are shaking. You're a doctor. You ought to know. You have dope in you, whether you are using or someone is giving it to you in such a way you don't know. What have you eaten tonight?"

Marty could tell he had made sense. Moe was thinking. He involuntarily looked over at a casserole with about half of it gone. "Moe, they are not your friends."

"There you go again. You come in here and accuse them of stealing. I asked them about the Chinese plate, by the way. They haven't seen it but said you always liked it—so maybe you'd taken it."

"Now ain't that great? Why in the world would I take a plate I've been looking at for forty years? They're doing a number on you, and you better wake up before the lights go out."

Moe had always been the bright one, but the one who could get lost in the dark. Marty couldn't help himself; he stood up and walked over placing his arm around Moe's shoulder.

Moe screamed, "Leave me alone. Get out of here and leave me alone."

Marty was stung. His first thought was to slug him in the gut, make him see. That wouldn't be fair because even thought Moe was a full six inches taller, he was nowhere as strong as Marty. Marty started walking from the room, stopped suddenly and retraced his steps. He put a spoonful of the casserole in a paper towel.

He didn't know how to test it, but Doug could probably find someone in the police department to see if the Hendrickses were doping Moe. Marty stopped to call Doug but got no answer. "Damn. Now I remember. He's on a run across country. He won't be back till Friday." This couldn't wait till then. He needed to know now. He'd have to go to the police himself. He had no idea whom he could trust. Would the old friends of Alvin Dozier kick his butt out of the station? Would they have already heard about the embezzlement and think of him as a suspect? Maybe they'd take the opportunity to arrest him. It was a chance he'd have to take.

Chapter Twenty-Four

There's never any great risk
as long as you have money.
E.M. Forster

Marty tried to pull himself up to his full five feet, five inches and hide his limp. The Marion Police Department sat in back of a huge parking lot, as unglamorous as a scab on a face wound. Prominently attached was the jail that probably housed an average of a half dozen different lawbreakers per week. Marty had never visited the police station but knew the location by passing it many times. He had a somewhat nervous cough before he approached the desk and then asked to talk to someone who might have already been approached by Mr. Doug Dozier. He realized his request was rambling but once he started, he couldn't very well stop and say let me start over.

"Doug Dozier, huh?" the officer said looking him over but not giving any signals as to what he was thinking, how he was measuring him up. "You kin to Doug? You kinda resemble him?"

Marty wasn't sure what he should say, what would Doug want him to say. Would Doug be humiliated if the department knew his dad's unfaithfulness had produced an illegitimate son? Would it stigmatize Doug with his acquaintances here?

What was the safest answer he could give?

He laughed. "We must be spending too much time together if we're growing to look alike."

The officer laughed too, and it eased the tension of first meeting and first impressions. "That would be Lukie. And you know what? Lukie stepped out for a minute. He's not here right now."

Marty was getting the runaround. He felt that he'd come to a dead end. The officer was brushing him off, and he'd have to wait for Doug to do the talking. "Well—" He was nodding his head, thinking, showing his disappointment when the door opened behind him.

"You just got in luck. Here's the man himself." Then he looked up at the officer entering the room. "Lukie, this here fellow is a friend of Doug's. You talked to him about a possible case the other day, didn't you? This man has something to add. I guess you did, didn't you? Anyway, he wants to talk to you."

"Sure, come on back to my little cubby hole. I had to run home for a national disaster. My wife will not take out the trash. She will let it sit and accumulate until it becomes a federal offense if I don't take it out." His argument had been presented so many times, he didn't have to think about what he was saying, Marty thought. But it gave a framework to this man that Doug evidently trusted. These policemen were on the level after all.

Marty explained in nebulous terms his suspicion that the "certain parties" are slipping drugs into "another certain party's" food, and he'd brought in a sample to have it analyzed. Luke, a young officer, handsome as a movie star, took the paper towel of food and pulled open a file folder that lay on the side of his desk. "Doug gave me a run down of what you suspect is happening to Dr. Lackey. You are Marty Price, aren't you? I could tell because you resemble Doug. Doug told me all about it. And I've been checking on a few things today. "

Marty instantly like Lukie's honesty and how easily he made him feel comfortable. "Yeah?"

"Yeah. Did you know Dr. Lackey had contacted his lawyer about changing some very important documents? His life insurance beneficiary and his will?"

"How do you know that? I've never had knowledge whatsoever of any of his personal business like that. Mrs. Violet handled all that kind of stuff."

"Well, Mrs. Violet has recently been admitted to a nursing home in Georgetown, am I right? And am I right in assuming she went for psychological testing for being mentally impaired? Right?"

Luke's words were beginning to paint an ugly picture in Marty's mind. "Yes, I suppose that's right. I don't really understand all you are saying, but it could be that if Mrs. Violet is found crazy—"

"Right! Bingo! If she is found incompetent, everything goes to the son, the only heir, the doctor.

"Oh, and another important factor," continued Lukie, leaning back in his chair. "We've had our eye on Coach Hendricks for quite some time. It's a shame, a damn shame—a man so highly respected in the region, in this state—like, how many years has he coached basketball? He was coaching when I played for Dillon. Since he retired, even before he retired, we found out, he'd been hitting the video poker machines pretty heavy. He's got a pattern. He makes the circuit;

he goes over to South of the Border, Dillon, Green Sea, Longs, Myrtle Beach. A lot of people believe that the machines will only let you win once in a blue moon, so he goes from one joint to another. Once in a while he goes up to Cherokee Casino up near Lancaster. He's lost a ton of money, and he's getting deeper and deeper. He's mortgaged his house, and it's very likely he will lose it. They go to the car shows when they have a win. That's to keep his wife happy. I doubt she really knows the scope of things, but maybe she does, and that's why she's in on it. It's all about money with those two.

"We've seen this happen before," he went on. "A person has a win or two, and then they can't get enough. It's a gambling addiction. It traps a person. Especially a man like coach who's been busy all his life, and now he's a has-been. Too much time on his hands. Smart enough to think he can lick the gamblers but dumb enough not to know when to quit. Sad."

"Does Doug know you know all this?"

"We've talked, but he's concerned they might try something drastic with the doctor since you got in the picture They know you'll figure it out, and that's the problem. We've been keeping a tab on his activities with the gambling, and now he's dabbling in drugs."

"You know about the rumors they've already started?" Marty voice was weak.

"Oh, that. People don't care about some of that anymore. What you do in private is your own business."

"But—"

"What concerns us is not even the way he's trying to put the blame on you— but they might just be plotting murder."

"Murder?"

Lukie watched the expression on Marty's face for a few minutes. "Damn, if it ain't funny how much you and Doug look alike. Let me tell you something, Marty, the men here, the oldtimers, they knew Dozier. They've said what a rounder he was in his younger days, but he settled down after awhile. But who knows, they might even be more of you out there somewhere."

Chapter Twenty-Five

A wise person should have money in their head,
but not in their heart.

Jonathan Swift

Marty tossed his weak leg from one side of the bed to the other, trying to find a comfortable enough position that sleep would come. But his thoughts were too many. Every time he tried to sleep, he remembered something else about the life he and Moe had shared. Not much of a life, just two people trying to make sense of a rotten world. Trying to make the best of fates that had always seemed predetermined. Moe's fate had been preordained before he ever learned his name.

And his own? Aunt Blanche had a future planned for him, one that was way above his ability to accomplish. His parents never had any ideas of a future for him. His biological father never even knew he existed, and his mother never had a plan for her own life, much less his. She just wanted the same for him as her—survival in this world. His granddad never had a plan, and his grandmother, bless her, she had some notion of Scotland and the old way. In all the tossing and turning and hitting his pillow, he knew one thing: He had to do whatever it took to keep Moe from the clutches of the Hendrickses.

All his life, he'd been hyper conscious of the injustices in the world, and he'd tried but never really been able to balance the scales for anyone. Not his mother, not Korea. Now he had a chance to do something for Moe, but could he? Could he do something in time? Would it be enough? Would Moe let him? He and Moe were basically two sides of the same coin. Why was Marty so intent on saving Moe from the Hendrickses? He couldn't answer that. Moe had basically been a bad influence on others. Ironically, he'd never expressed one iota of a belief in humanity or God. The whole lot of Lackeys, for that matter—what had they ever done for Britton's Neck or anyone else? Sure, Mrs. Violet came out of her shell when it benefitted Moe. But when else had she ever reached out to others? Never. He couldn't speculate on Moe's father. Moe told him his dad had wanted to be a soldier, but what had he actually ever done? They gave the town a doctor, but did Moe really care if his patients lived or died? He had never once heard him speak of one of them with endearment, with compassion. The entire family seemed heartless, robots.

And what did Mrs. Violet mean the night the ambulance came for her when she said something about her long gone daughter? It was as if she expected her daughter to still be alive. What had she said, something about them giving her back? He was certain she had said that. Who was she talking about? Okay, he decided, he'd go straight to Georgetown, find Mrs. Violet and ask her. Go straight to the horse's mouth—that had always been his motto.

Decisions could be made in the midst of turbulent sleep. Like wringing out right answers from God. If you fight him long enough, he just might help you, he told himself. Now, what about Moe?

The next morning he overlooked the Ford Pinto that had

been sitting in his garage for two days. He knew he could fix it in a couple hours and would do so later today. He asked his Aunt Blanche to find out the name of the nursing home. When she called him back, he could tell she really wanted to go with him—probably for protection. He wanted to work alone and not involve his aunt with details that would only make her jump into action, perhaps prematurely. It was at least a thirty-minute drive and his mind was racing, trying to organize his questions in categories so as not to upset Mrs. Violet in her condition. Could he even discuss with her, he wondered, about the Hendrickses? Should she even know about the danger Moe was in? No, he decided it would be too much for her in her mental state to broach that subject. Just try to act normal, like it was a friendly visit.

He was expecting the nursing home to be similar to the dilapidated one Alvin Dozier was in, but was amazed that the facility was modern. The landscaping was professionally done—trees and shrubbery and flowers and benches and bird feeders and a fake waterfall that patients could see from their windows. There was no odor to greet him but bustling nurses and attendants. He was given a name card and directions. He expected to see a mentally deranged Mrs. Violet, but heard her voice before he ever entered the room. She sounded amazingly energetic. He walked in and saw she was sitting at the window and having a conversation with the attendant about the menu for dinner. When she looked up and saw Marty, she rose from her chair and came to him. "Martin, are you alone? Isn't Moses with you?" She was puzzled and disappointed he could tell.

"I didn't expect to see you looking so good, Mrs. Violet.

You're a sight for sore eyes."

"Well, thank you. You are too. But I don't know why my son hasn't been to see me. Do you?"

"No'um I don't. He hasn't been?"

Evidently she knew nothing much about the nature of things back at the mansion. He wondered how much she knew about the Hendrickses. He couldn't believe this was the same person he had seen last.

"They must be got you on some kind of medicine," he said.

"Actually, I've never felt better. They said I had been on too much medication. And, you know, Martin, that's strange. I only take my blood pressure medicine that Moe prescribed for me. Once in awhile I take a little One-A-Day vitamin. They've made me rest and get back in the habit of eating well. You know, Martin, it's hard to eat when you are alone. The only thing I was eating lately is the little bit that Mrs. Hendricks brought me."

Marty now saw more of the whole picture. Her illness and staying in her room all the time was from the drugs they were putting in her food. "Have they been down here to see you, Mrs. Violet?"

"No, not yet. No one from home has been, but you, now. But that's the way it is. I don't socialize that much really. I don't expect anyone to visit—that is, except Moe."

He wanted to say that Moe was not well himself but didn't want to upset her. He tried to chitchat but wasn't too good at small talk. He wanted to get around to asking about her statement about her lost daughter.

"Mrs. Violet, your husband has family down here in

Georgetown, doesn't he? Have any of them been to see you?

"The Lackeys. They're dying out, Martin. Davis's family. Used to be so many of them. I felt—oh well, you don't want to hear about them." She looked as if a shadow had come over her and turned her face to the window again, looking out.

"But I do like to hear about stuff like that. It's interesting. You know all the years Moe and me were growing up I never came not one time with y'all down here to see the family. And he's never once said a word about the family."

"Well, it's a long story, and I don't want to talk about it today. I'm just so glad you've come," her tone changed to the brightness it had earlier. "Tell me about Blanche. How's your aunt?"

"Aunt Blanche wanted to come along with me today."

"Well, I wish you had insisted that she come. Your mother and I were as close as anyone. I guess that's why you and Moe became good friends, don't you?"

"Yes'um, I reckon so. Look, Mrs. Violet, this is very important. First of all, if the Hendrickses come to visit you, do not see them alone, and do not, I repeat, do not eat anything they bring you. It's very important."

"Martin, please. What are you talking about? Why are you suddenly so concerned about the Hendrickses?"

"Mrs. Violet, please, just do as I say. Please."

"Well, we'll see." She spoke with her aristocratic ambiguity.

"And," he waited and sat near her, "Mrs. Violet, what did you mean about your daughter—when you said you thought they'd give her back."

The cloud came over her clear blue eyes once again. "Oh.

Did I say that? I don't remember saying that. I must have been dreaming. Or maybe you misunderstood."

"No, ma'am. The night the ambulance took you to the hospital. You said you thought they'd bring her back. What did you mean? Who took her, Mrs. Violet?"

"Martin, my heart. I need to see a nurse. Would you get one for me, please."

Marty saw that her countenance had changed like day to night. Was Mrs. Violet about to have a heart attack? He stepped out into the hall and saw an attendant coming from another room and asked that she come immediately.

Before they had walked the short distance to the room, Mrs. Violet had locked the door by putting a chair beneath the door handle. "Mrs. Lackey! Mrs. Lackey! Open the door." The attendant ran to a nurse's station and spoke in a low voice to the nurse who immediately picked up the phone and then walked quickly back to the room. An orderly met her at the door and began removing the door.

"Young man, I'm afraid I've have to ask you to wait here in the hall," said the nurse. She and the attendant entered the room. Marty watched as an older doctor with a silver mane of hair rushed down the hall and into the room. There was hushed discussion and then a scream, "No, I've been doing well! Do not give me anything! I'll be calm." More hushed talk that Marty could not understand.

Then the doctor came out of the room and stopped. His piercing black eyes looked intently at Marty. "You were with Mrs. Lackey. Please come with me."

He followed the doctor as best he could, but he was moving rapidly down the hall and entered a small office just beyond the nurse's station. The doctor was already scanning Mrs. Violet's file at the time Marty entered the office as if his life depended on it. He then looked up to Marty and demanded, "What had you said to Mrs. Lackey to cause her to have this panic attack?"

"I was trying to warn her about some—er—people who might try to harm her. I can't go into it with you—except to say that they might have given her drugs and may try to again. But, you see, I don't have any proof. I'd just like for you to see that she doesn't have visitors."

"Right now you're the only visitor I'm worried about trying to harm her!"

"Yeah, I guess it kinda looks like that. But there was something else that I asked her right before she started to –er—have the panic attack. You might not know it, but she had—has—a girl—a woman now, I suppose, if she's still alive. But her girl ran off years ago and, well, when Mrs. Violet, Mrs. Lackey, the night she was taken away from her home all messed up, she said she hoped they'd bring her girl back. You see, it sounded like there might have been something other than a runaway-teenager years ago. Don't it to you?"

"And you asked Mrs. Lackey about some statement she said on the night she was half out of her mind with drugs and alcohol? Do you really think you can attach any credibility to her words under those circumstances?"

"Since you put it like that... Hey, but when she saw me, she had a recollection of my mother. That was pretty sane, don't you think?"

"I have no way of knowing how the two could be connected." When he turned to show Marty out, Marty noticed something he'd missed—the name stitched in the doctor's jacket: LACKEY. He was about to ask about it, but the doctor had placed his hand on Marty's shoulder forcefully to escort him out. "I don't think it's a good idea for you to visit Mrs. Lackey in the future. Your presence and inquiries into unpleasant family events from the past cause grave consequences. Now, if you'd excuse me, I'll say goodbye so that you can leave."

Marty was being ramrodded out of the nursing home, and he didn't like it. Who was this Dr. Lackey who didn't want him interfering in Mrs. Violet's life? And why? *Best to pretend to know nothing and get out of here for now,* he thought. He walked to his Impala and sat there letting his mind settle before starting it. He rubbed his hands back and forth on the red leather interior as if to make his thoughts produce answers. Who could help him know what was going on with these Lackeys? Mrs. Violet had said they were dying out. Well, here's one who wasn't dead yet but very much alive and in control of her life and wanting him out of it.

Maybe it was time to talk to Aunt Blanche.

Chapter Twenty-Six

Money can only give happiness where
there is nothing else to give it.

Jane Austen

"Now you have to promise me you won't say anything to anybody about what I'm gonna tell you, okay?" Marty implored.

"Is it all that serious, Marty?" Blanche wanted to hold him and hug away his troubled look. Over the years her body had taken on a plumpness that his mother's never had. Aunt Blanche's hair, which had once been a beautiful auburn, was now streaked with white, and she had taken to wearing it shorter and close to her face. Since she'd gotten into Christianity, she had a natural glow about her face as if angels' reflections were bouncing off of it. "I swear to God," he'd say to people about the angels' reflections when describing her new countenance.

"Promise me."

"All right, I promise."

"Tell me what you know about the Lackeys. There's something crazy about that family, and I think right now Mrs. Violet is in danger big time."

"You know how the Lackeys have always been—elite-ish, aloof, away from everyone else. I doubt I know anymore than you—if as much as you. You've been there with Moe. You and Moe kinda grew up together. Tell me what's got you so worried."

"Well, in the first place—I don't hardly know where to start." He wanted to get all the details in the right order and say everything so Blanche would understand the gravity of it all but not insist on doing something drastic. "Actually there're two different situations going on, see?" Blanche was nodding as if trying to follow every syllable. "First, there are the teachers who are trying to take over the Lackey place—now, Aunt Blanche, this is very important that you don't tell anybody this—it could mean someone's life. Okay?" She nodded. "They are drugging Moe and were drugging Mrs. Violet until she got so bad, she had to go to the Georgetown Rehabilitation Hospital. Then they got her cleaned out, and she was doing fine until—" He felt he was not being very clear. He desperately wished he were smarter so he could explain things better.

"Marty, until what?"

"You see, the night they took her in the ambulance, she said to me. She said she wished they would bring her daughter back. Just like she knew her daughter was not dead or had not run away but that someone had taken her. I know that's what she meant. But when I asked her about it today at the hospital, she went into hysterics and locked herself in the room. Then they had to get the janitor to take the door off, and a doctor came and gave her a shot to knock her out and, Aunt Blanche, he was a *Dr. Lackey*. And he told me to leave and not come back. To, more or less, stay away from Mrs. Violet. Now ain't that a hell of a—I mean, something is wrong here. Anyone can see that."

"Martin, I think you're right. If what you are telling me is the truth—and I do believe you, mind you—something is out of kilter." She turned her head away as if she was struggling to think. After a few seconds, she stood and walked over to the coat closet and reached to the shelf above the few jackets and a raincoat hanging in the closet. She moved a few books and magazines around and pulled out an old scrapbook.

"There's something in here—I haven't looked at this for years. The article that was in the paper."

She brushed off some dust and opened up the oversized black scrapbook with the word *Memories* in a flowing script. Yellowed newspapers clippings had been glued down to the black construction paper pages. He'd never seen the scrapbook and could only wonder at what his aunt might have found interesting enough to glue to the stiff pages. There were articles with photos of her promotions at the phone company—many of them. There were the obituaries of his grandfather Winston Price, his grandmother Nadine Price, and her husband Harold Fitzgibbons. His mother's obituary wouldn't be in the scrapbook, he knew; it was in a gold-colored double frame—a school photo of her in her white cafeteria uniform was in one side of the frame and the obituary in the other. Other pages held clippings with photographs of Dr. Lackey opening his office, Vereen's Drugstore opening, and the Williams when they opened the first restaurant in Britton's Neck. Marty and Aunt Blanche were bent over the scrapbook reading the headlines as Blanche kept turning the pages. Finally she came to a page with the headlines Prominent Upstate Senator Wants Answers. The article was written about Hazeline Lackey.

Blanche began to read it aloud.

> A prominent member of the South Carolina Senate is rousing local Marion County officials to extend their investigation into the alleged run away of Hazeline Lackey, 16 year-old-daughter of Mr. and Mrs. Davis Lackey of Britton's Neck. "It is not possible that this beautiful, intelligent young girl would just up and disappear from the face of God's green earth," said Elliott Knotts Bradley of Spartanburg. Local sheriff's deputies reportedly have been in touch with police departments as far away as New York City and California hoping to find a trace of Miss Lackey."

"Aunt Blanche, this senator? Why would he get involved? I think I remember something Moe told me about his mother had to contact someone in her family to pull strings to get me shipped home when I was wounded in Korea. Do you know who he is?"

"I can very well find out—that is, if he's still alive."

"It would help if we could get Moe on our side, but he's so wrapped up with the Hendrickses right now that—"

"Hendrickses? Are they the teachers you were referring to? I knew it. I knew something was going on with them. You know you have a gut feeling about people sometimes. And since I've been saved, I've prayed the Lord would forgive me for my negative feelings toward them."

"Doug will be back Friday from his trucking to California. He had to take a load and bring a load back. He's got men in the police department working on this, and they already knew about Coach. But, I swear, Aunt Blanche, you can't tell not one soul about this. You can't even pray out loud about them. It could mean someone could get killed."

"Oh, Marty. Do you think they are that dangerous?"

"I wouldn't have thought so before, but now I believe that money will drive some people to murder or worse!"

Chapter Twenty-Seven

Money often costs too much.

Ralph Waldo Emerson

Doug's return could not come soon enough. The Pinto still sat in the shop for Marty to work on. He'd fixed it enough times already he could do so in his sleep. Then Doug called to say that he would not be back Friday. The load he was to bring back to South Carolina was a partial load; he'd have to pick up the rest in another state. This sometimes happens. Marty didn't want to make Doug feel bad about his job, but he couldn't help blurting out that things were happening pretty damn quick and another angle had come into play that was making matters ever stickier.

"Don't try to do anything till I get back. We need to stick together. You might get hurt," said Doug. The phone connection wasn't all that clear, and Marty knew the cost for a long distance call was steep, so he just told him to be careful and keep his nose clean and hung up.

Every muscle in his body was twitching. His old wounds hurt more when it rained or when he was extremely tense. He knew he needed to make sure Moe was all right. What if the Hendrickses overdrugged him to the point of death? Was he able to open his office every day? How was he able to function? That was it—he'd go to the office as a patient and see him that way. And he and Aunt Blanche—or just Aunt Blanche could go check on Miss Violet—his mind was racing and he had to make it slow down. This he knew: He couldn't wait until Doug got back to South Carolina. It might be too late!

He rushed past the disabled Pinto on his way to his Impala and headed out to the doctor's office. Every business in the world seemed to close up on Wednesday afternoon. Always had, still did, and always would. The doctor's office was no exception. It would close at 1:00 on the dot.

The nurse-receptionist looked up from where she sat on the other side of the thin paneled wall and stuck the clipboard through the window for him to sign in. She looked to be about twenty years old, but he knew she had to be older than that. He didn't know her, but that wasn't any surprise. He tried not to know many people. "So the doc is working today?"

"Yes, sir. Sign your name if you want to be seen. He's not too terribly busy today."

Marty jotted his name on the line below two other names on the pad in the clipboard and kept looking back toward the door leading to the examining rooms. As customs in small places are only changed by force or radical idealists, whites went down a short hall to the examining rooms on the right side of the office and colored went on the left even though segregation laws had changed in the South ten years earlier. Marty kept looking back at the door as if he'd go right on through.

"You can sit down." The nurse said, matter-of-factly. She has no idea who I am, he thought.

He looked at his watch and at the coffee table with the magazines, not aware of what his actions would be, just wanting to see Moe but still not knowing what he was going to say to him. He wondered how Aunt Blanche would make out with Mrs. Violet.

Later, he reflected on what transpired between him and Moe, who was livid that Marty had taken up his time and on a half day to get information. He felt sure the nurse and other patients could hear Moe's rumbling voice, trying to keep it down, but it didn't work. Marty, in his khakis and Army tee shirt, stormed out of the office without even stopping to look at the nurse-receptionist.

He fumbled as he worked under the Pinto's hood and then started the engine to hear it purr like a kitten. He called the owner's work number and told him it was ready. Then he called Blanche but got no answer. He was about to walk outside when the phone rang as if on cue.

"Marty, didn't you tell me Violet was in Georgetown Rehabilitation Hospital? Is there more than one?"

"After you get off 521, it's one mile down on 17."

"They told me no one was there by the name of Violet Lackey. When I asked to speak to Dr. Lackey, they said he had retired and could not be reached."

"I'll be darn. Something real fishy is going on, Aunt Blanche. You come on home. I tried to see Moe at his office and batted zero. He more or less kicked me out."

"I tell you what, I'm going to try to get back in the nursing home and look around."

"I'll head down that way. See you in thirty-five minutes. If you don't find out anything, go to the McDonalds and wait for me. I'll ride by there first."

Thirty-five minutes later, Marty pulled in beside Blanche's

car at McDonalds.

"So, were you able to find out anything else," Marty asked jumping in her car.

"I was able to slip in without being noticed and went to the room you said. It was empty so I went in and looked through the dresser, nightstand—nothing—not a thread of Violet's. I started going to rooms of patients beside her room, and—it's sometimes hard to talk to senile people—and not a one of them could understand who I was looking for. I wanted to ask an attendant but didn't know if I could trust her."

"Were you able to find the office he took me to the yesterday?"

"Yes, I pretending I was looking for a patient. I even held a card with a room number written on it."

"Did you look just beyond the nurse's station on the right?"

"Marty, I looked in every room on both sides of the hall, down one side and up the other. There was nothing that looked like an office."

"We'll go back together. Like you did, pretend we are looking for another patient. We've got to find her and find out about that Dr. Lackey—who he is, where he lives, then we'll go there."

"Marty, I have a crazy idea. Why don't we pretend you want to admit me to the nursing home? Like you're my son, and I'm becoming an invalid. It's crazy, but we might be able to find out something."

"It is crazy. If they call our bluff, we can just walk out."

Each of them tried to reassure the other to be cool and act natural, but both of them thought they'd be recognized and asked why they were back. They approached the desk, and Marty said, "I need to see about having my mother here put in here because she is becoming feeble-minded."

The receptionist looked from Marty to Blanche, "Has a doctor sent you here?"

"He didn't have to. Everyone knows she's getting more forgetful all the time. She can't remember her name some times. Forgets if she has eaten."

"I'm sorry you can't just walk in and have someone admitted without a doctor's referral."

Marty was about to step back and leave, but Blanche stepped forward. "I've gone down so badly lately; I feel sure my doctor will give a referral, and my son wants me to come to this nursing facility because it's the best in the area. Before that happens, and while I am thinking coherently today and might not be tomorrow, I'd like to look around to see the place, if you don't mind. I'd like to see where I might be spending the rest of my days." Blanche talked sweetly and looked her best Christian self at the receptionist, looking her straight in the eyes.

The receptionist smiled her sweetest smile back at Blanche and spoke as she would to a small child, "Of course, I can show you around and then when your doctor signs a referral, we'll look forward to having you." She started to rise.

"I wouldn't want to interrupt your work. My son and I will just walk down the hall and look at the rooms to see what I can bring of my personal belongings when I come. I'd like to see the cafeteria and the day room, if you don't mind."

"Yes, of course, you just take your time, Mrs.—"

"Fitzgibbons."

As she and Marty walked down the hall, Blanche tried to impersonate a person who was much older and might be mentally incapacitated. Marty even put out his arm to support her. They walked down the hall where Violet's room had been, trying to act as if that room were not the one in focus. They looked in several rooms on the other side of the hall and then entered the room where Violet had been. There were now two occupants, but the curtain was drawn blocking the view of the second occupant.

Blanche spoke softly to the elderly lady who sat in the first bed, "Hello, I'm going to be coming here soon. I used to have a friend, Mrs. Violet Lackey, here but I can't find her. Have you seen her?"

"Eh? What you say?" The lady looked agitated. Apparently, she hadn't understood one word Blanche had said.

Blanche spoke a bit louder but still restrained, "I am looking for an old friend—Mrs. Violet Lackey. Do you know her?"

"What?" the woman screamed.

"They came and took her in the middle of the night and took her out the back way," came a squeaky voice from the second bed, which was behind the curtain.

Blanche and Marty looked at each other. "Do you mind if I visit with you for a minute?" asked Blanche as she slowly approached and drew back the curtain. The tiny frame of a dried up lady lay on the bed, a homemade quilt folded at her feet and a thin hospital spread pulled up to her neck. Her white hair was sprawled on her pillow and a tuff of hair on her chin, a goatee, seemed pronounced because of her elfish facial features. So did her eyes seem to protrude looking larger than normal for such a small face.

"Do you mind pulling up my quilt? I'm freezing cold. They won't be back in here for another hour."

Blanche carefully tucked the quilt around the petite frame and smiled. "So you knew my friend, Mrs. Violet? I wish I had known they were going to move her. Do you know who moved her, and where she is now? Was it Dr. Lackey?"

"*Doctor* Lackey? My eye! He ain't no doctor! He's a patient."

"Did he take my friend? She didn't tell me she wanted to go to another place."

"She didn't. She was happy here except for missing her son. She wanted to go home to see him. He ain't even been to see her since she first day she got her. He did like lots of folks, bring 'em and forget 'em. She made excuses like most of them saying he must be busy, or he must be sick."

"Well, he is sick, and I'm sure he wants to come visit. Just like us. This is my son and he will visit me when I come."

"No, he won't. He's the one who came to visit Mrs. Violet and made her so mad."

"Oh, he had to ask her some questions because he knew they might move her. Can you tell me more about why they moved her and where? I really want to see her."

The little elf of a lady turned to stare out the window at the glistening water of the waterfall. "I wouldn't tell the other folks, and I don't see why I need to tell you either."

"The other folks? When did they come?" Marty had drawn up close to his Aunt Blanche and nudged her shoulder. "Do you mean the man and his wife?"

"Yes ma'am. She called him Ken. They were here this morning early. I didn't tell them not one thing. Told them if they didn't see her, she must not be here."

"I'm glad you didn't tell them because they're not her friends. We are. We really need to know so we can help her. She might be in trouble."

"She is in trouble. *Doctor* Lackey and his other friend came in the middle of the night—after he had given her that shot to make her sleep. They just up and loaded her in a wheelchair and snuck out the back. He gets away with whatever he wants to do in here. You better watch him. He ain't no doctor, I tell you."

"Thank you for telling me. How do you know all this?"

"I was in the room across the hall, and I can't sleep. I haven't slept in years. I heard them two coming and trying to be quiet. And then he told the girl, 'Get this room changed and move people in her. Get every trace of her outta here and off the records—tonight!"

"Oh my goodness. I hate to hear this for Mrs. Violet's sake. She's such a nice, sweet lady."

"She can be, but she can be stuck up too. At first when she came in here she wouldn't have a thing to do with anybody. Then she started to like it, having good meals and all."

"I didn't even ask your name. I'm sorry," said Blanche reaching over patting the quilt where her arm would be.

"Everybody calls me Little Bit but my given name is Gwendolyn Rose. You can call me whatever. When do you think you'll be coming in here?"

Blanche's tender heart and her new Christian conscious made her hang her head slightly.

The sage noticed this, "You really ain't coming in here at all, are you? You just wanted to find out about Mrs. Violet, didn't you?"

"We must find her, Gwendolyn, she's in danger. Please tell us if you know where they took her. And please do not give us away if anyone asks about us. Mrs. Violet is in danger from the other couple who came here, and now I fear she might be in danger from this Doctor Lackey."

"Honey, I could look at you and your son—if he is your son—and tell you are honest people even if you are trying to use dishonest means to get to the truth. I can tell when people are good on the inside. He has the biggest house on Bay Street. If you go there, remember what I say: Watch out for him. He may be a doctor, but he ain't a real doctor."

Footsteps were coming nearer. Blanche rose and neared Marty.

"Little Bit, it's time for your medicine."

"Eh, what you say?" She winked at Blanche and Marty and turned to the attendant who handed her a pill and a glass of water.

"Here you go, Sug," said the nurse who then turned and left the room, looking over Blanche and Marty carefully as she exited.

Little Bit took the pills from her mouth and stuck them in a little bag in her nightstand drawer. "They'd keep us knocked out all the time if we took all the stuff they shove at us. If you find Mrs. Violet before they do something bad to her, tell her Little Bit said 'Hey.'"

As they walked down the hall, Marty urged Blanche to show him where she'd gone looking for the doctor's office. She wanted to leave, but he insisted, thinking she must have gone to the wrong place.

"Okay, but I'm ready to get out of here," she whispered. She acted as if he were trying to help her find the cafeteria and the day room, leading her by the arm. He took her directly to the room Dr. Lackey had taken him. "This *is* the place I came," she said.

Marty was stunned. The office was completely different. There was no sign that it had ever been an office. "Yeah, let's get out of here."

"Were you looking for something in particular?" said the same attendant who had given Little Bit her pills.

"Just checking out the place," Marty said. "But we've seen enough. I think she'll be happy here, won't you, Mother?"

Blanche felt they should leave quickly and return to Britton's Neck and wait for reinforcements; however, Marty said they should not wait. Doug would not be back until the weekend. It would take too long to wait for Luke, the police officer. They should try to locate the house over on the bay and see if they could come up with a plan to get inside. Blanche reluctantly gave in to Marty. He was braver than she had imagined. They left her car in a parking lot and headed for the bay area where Little Bit had said the doctor lived. They drove to the bay area and easily found Bay Street, which was closest to the water. All the homes were huge multimillion-dollar mansions. Then they saw it. There was a brick fence around the property with double entrances through which they could see the sprawling house nestled among the mossy live oaks, long needle pines, sago palms, azaleas, and palmettos. It looked like a fortress, but through the flora, you could see glimpses of the bay.

When Marty started to turn his Impala between the

pillars, Blanche pulled on his arm. "Marty, the doctor has seen you. I'll have to be the one to go to the door. I don't think I can do this. I'm afraid."

"Aunt Blanche, the doctor is most likely not even here, maybe a maid. All you'll have to do is make up some reason to be here and then look around as best you can to see if you spot Mrs. Violet."

"But what can I say?"

"You're smarter than me. Maybe you can say you are taking a survey or looking to buy a home in the area, or—I got it—you can say you are taking water samples because people have complained about too much chlorine or fluoride or whatever they put in city water."

"In that case maybe we better go to all the houses. Maybe we can get a feel for the neighborhood."

"I told you, you were smarter!" He said as he backed out and pulled into the driveway next to the Lackey house.

Marty had to smile as he watched his Aunt Blanche walking up to the door of a house that cost more than half the houses in Britton's Neck altogether. She smoothed her hair and adjusted her handbag and rang the doorbell. She waited and rang it again. Still no answer. After about three houses, a maid did come to the door and looked aggravated to have an unannounced caller. "We don't wish to participate," she said stonily.

"It's mandatory and will save me time if I can get the sample today. It will only take a moment."

"Oh, all right. Come in. Where is your sample container? And could you give me a card of some kind to show the homeowners when they ask about it?"

"Oh dear, I do believe I'll have to run and come back later. I forgot a prior appointment."

After she got in the car, she said she was losing faith in the idea. She felt the maid was suspicious and would probably warn the other neighbors. "Aw, these people probably don't even know one another. Look how many of them ain't even home. Just go up and ring the doorbell and ask if you're at the house of—make up a name."

"But that won't get me in the house."

"No, but we'll see if anyone is at home."

"Oh, Marty, let's don't do this."

"You can do it, Aunt Blanche. Now, we're gonna do it, okay? Get ready."

She had already been through enough for one day by pretending to be mentally deficient at the nursing home, but she was prepared to pretend a bit more as she rang the doorbell. Almost immediately the door opened and there stood the tall, silver-haired doctor Marty had described. His piercing eyes were scrutinizing her. "Come in, please. Whatever you are selling, I will listen to your sales pitch, but I'm not sure I'll buy."

She wanted to retrace her steps, but he was debonair, and he had reached for her hand, pulling her inside the open room. She had no time to think or gain her composure. He was completely in control.

"Here, have a seat. Let me ring for you a drink. What shall you have? Too early for a martini. Iced tea, perhaps?"

"Water, if you have a glass of water."

He rang a bell and a maid appeared from a side room off from the palatial living room, decorated in white sofas and beige and azure rugs. A columned fireplace with a gigantic portrait of a beautiful woman above it demanded attention and through the open living room was a dining room with an ecru dining table and matching padded Chippendale chairs with a low hanging globed chandelier above. "Would your partner also like to come inside?" Doctor Lackey asked with a knowing look, as he pulled back his pale green polyester jacket that matched his plaid polyester slacks.

"No, my driver is waiting, and I really must hurry. I just wanted to ask about the neighborhood, especially the water. We'll be taking water samples in a few days. Have you any complaints about fluoride in your drinking water?"

"Here you are," he said, handing her a glass of iced water. "Maybe you can tell yourself if the water is satisfactory."

Blanche took the glass and napkin handed her and welcomed a sip. "Thank you."

"Now, what do you think? Do you think we can cut out this little game and get down to why you are really here, Mrs. 'Mentally-Declining' Fitzgibbons?" The stare from his piercing eyes put a chill through her.

Blanche breathed a silent prayer of three words, "Lord, help me." And at the next instance, she heard the knock at the door. Doctor Lackey shifted his gaze from her to the door.

"Let's see who we have here," he said with a voice of steel as he walked to the door. He looked at Marty with a grin, "It is the visitor who was so concerned about other visitors wanting to harm Mrs. Lackey. You two appear to be going to much trouble to get to Mrs. Lackey. I wonder why."

Marty looked over to make sure his Aunt Blanche was safe. "We know you are up to something, *Doctor* Lackey. And we aim to find out what you have done with Mrs. Violet. You moved her out of the nursing home. Now where in hell is she? What have you done with her?"

"You are making some strong accusations, young man. For someone who is scavenging the neighborhood under false pretenses, claiming to be checking the water, for God's sake! Maybe I'd better just call the police right now and have you both arrested for false impersonations."

"Yeah, why don't you do that? Go ahead. Call the police."

"If you two are so concerned about Mrs. Lackey," he began to turn away from them, "then I must tell you. Violet Lackey is my sister-in-law. I moved her for her own safety. You, and that other pair of God-knows-what or who have turned her life into a hellish nightmare. Her life is hanging by a thread apparently. People giving her drugs, alcohol—trying to kill her. I saw no other way but to move her here to give her the medical attention she so badly needs and remove her from harm's way."

"Sister-in-law? I don't believe you. And I don't believe you are trying to help her. We want to see her for ourselves. Where is she?"

"*That*—I will not tell you! That's why I moved her—to get her away from you. I can't reveal her sanctuary. She's safe, and if you really are friends trying to prevent further harm to her, you'll just have to trust me." He smiled at both of them. "Now, if you'd like to be on your way?"

"No, we don't want to be on our way—not just yet," growled Marty as he pugnaciously stepped toward the doctor.

Blanche inhaled deeply and stepped toward Marty, "I believe the doctor is right, Marty. Now, we need to trust him and leave his home for the time being." She reached for Marty's arm, as much to support herself as to apply pressure for him to move toward the door. Marty's immediate reaction was to shake off her hand and hound the doctor until he relented and took them to Mrs. Violet. The old Marty was being reincarnated, but he sensed the right thing to do was get Blanche out of the house.

As they drove away, he turned to her, "He's lying through his teeth."

"Yes, he is, but, Marty, before you came in, I saw that he was a very dangerous man. He *is* a dangerous man."

As they drove back to Britton's Neck in their separate cars, each of them reenacted the day's business, and each came to the conclusion: Mrs. Violet Lackey's life was in danger. Moe's life was in danger. It was critical that they do something. And quick!

Blanche fixed supper for Marty. Her maternal instincts rose within her breast. She'd always thought if she'd had a son, he would have been taller and smarter and would have fulfilled the potential she felt her son would achieve. Now as she floured and fried pork chops and stirred the lumps out of a pot of yellow grits, she knew with clarity that if she'd had a son, she would not have loved him any more than she loved Marty. "Want me to fry you an egg to go with your pork chop?" she asked, already cracking the shell. She'd quickly mixed up biscuit dough and had them baking and poured him a tall glass of iced sweet tea.

"Aunt Blanche, I don't ever remember Moe talking about an uncle—and a doctor. Don't you think if that man is his uncle and a doctor, he'd'a come to see them, especially with

Moe being a doctor and all? It's too strange to be true."

"There's a lot about this that doesn't meet the eye. It sounded to me like he has fabricating the story to keep us from calling the police. And the police are exactly where I think we need to go. I'll say again. I think he is a very dangerous man."

Chapter Twenty-Eight

There is only one class in the community that thinks more about money than the rich, and that is the poor.

Oscar Wilde

Marty had to visit Moe. He had to see him before he could finish off this crucial day. He drove from around the bay to the place where the only streetlights existed in Britton's Neck, for the length of a city block the power company had installed lights on either side of the highway around the doctor's office. For a few seconds, a passerby could imagine he or she was transported to a real town. Here on one side was the office of Dr. Moe Lackey in the foreground of the plantation house in the rear. On the other side of the street were Vereen's Drugstore, Williams' Restaurant, and Altman's Texaco. The Coca Cola Bottling Company had provided each of these businesses with a sign embellished with their business name free of charge.

Marty was pleased to see no other cars in front of the mansion except Moe's candy apple red Buick Rivera, so he pulled up behind it. As he walked to the door, he thought of the best way to begin the conversation about Mrs. Violet. As before, he knocked several times and waited. He got in his car and backed up as if to leave but decided he'd use the old driveway extension that led to a shed in the back. Years ago, horses and carriages occupied the shed, and one or two of the carriages was probably still in it buried in dust. He had not turned his car lights on and drove slowly and noiselessly to the back. He walked up to the wide patio that was the length of the entire house with several sets of patios doors. He crept like a burglar to each door and peered inside until his eyes adjusted to the dark interior, and he could make out familiar pieces of furniture.

One door led into the kitchen and the florescent light above the sink was burning, so he could easily ascertain no one was in the kitchen. Off from the kitchen he saw no one was in the dining room either. Another set of doors led into a moderately sized den with fireplace, its mantel hand hewn by slaves over one hundred years earlier. Matching brass candlesticks and ginger jars sat on the mantle, and an original brass spittoon sat now as simply decoration on the raised hearth. He saw no movement and didn't expect to as Moe rarely visited the antique room, as he called it, with the antique pump organ with Hazeline's photograph and frozen smile and the bookshelves holding antique volumes getting older and dustier every year. The last set of doors led to Mrs. Violet's room and the doors were covered with heavy lined draperies, tightly closed to block out any sunlight and the doors were double locked to keep the outside out and the inside in, he'd always heard Moe say. Thinking now of the saying, he wondered where Moe had picked up such a saying and why Moe would apply the saying to his mother's bedroom door.

Marty was about to leave the patio and to look in the end windows, when he heard muffled sounds coming from the bedroom. He pressed his ear to the glass yet still could not distinguish whose voice it was or what was being said. He carefully tried to move around the end of the house to look in a side window. The foundation of the house was built on the old order, high off the ground. There was no way Marty could see into the windows without a ladder. The dogwood tree closest to the window was ancient, but the limbs were strong enough to support him since he wasn't too heavy. With his crazy limp leg, he climbed up and tried to make out through the slit in the draperies whoever was inside. He couldn't tell. The drapery panels left only an inch of being tightly closed, and he was a good six feet from the window. He'd have to get inside the house.

He eased down from his perch in the tree and crept back to the patio. He'd have to force a door. Perhaps the kitchen door would be best since it was farthest away from the bedroom, and it would be least likely to be overheard. He took a flathead screwdriver from a small toolbox he always kept in the trunk of his car. The door slipped open easily, and he moved stealthily into the kitchen and then into the hall leading to Mrs. Violet's bedroom. Just as he entered the hall, he heard the voices getting louder.

The person who opened the bedroom door was still talking over his shoulder to another person in the room. Marty had to slide into the darkness of the den, the antique room. The bedroom door completely opened, and Coach Hendricks' huge body cast a silhouette on the wall.

"Don't let him regain consciousness, whatever you do. If he moves, give him another shot. It'll look like a heart attack. We've got his signature on here and that's all we need now. We are almost home free, baby!"

"When will you be back? I don't want to stay here all night with him. I still don't see why I can't take the document, and you stay here. If anything happens, I don't want to be found here." It was Mrs. Hendricks.

This was it. They were planning to murder him tonight—if he wasn't dead already.

"It's better this way, just like we planned it. Don't get squeamish now. He'll be gone before morning. One or two more shots will do it. We'll stick to our plan. This document is predated, and I know exactly where it needs to be, so there will never be a question about it. I'll be back here before daybreak to move him to his office. Now stay calm."

"But someone knocked on that door. I know I heard a knock."

"It's your nerves, baby. Nobody has been here. Nerves can do that to you. But if anyone should come, the house is locked up. I'm going now to move his car up to the office, so it'll look like he stayed there all night, working, working, working. Poor rich doctor worked himself to death. Ha. Ha. Found out his business was in the red, and he'd failed in his little scheme to get his fortune back."

"We still don't know about Mrs. Violet."

"Look, I tell you, baby, we take one step at a time. Finding her is next. It is already set in motion. This document settles it," he said as he kissed the folded papers in his hand and put them in his inside jacket pocket. "Now let me get out of here."

Marty pressed himself against the wall so as not to be heard. *What am I doing?* he suddenly thought. I need to stop him. He grabbed the brass candlestick and tried to ease up behind the Coach. Just as he was about to bring the candlestick down on Coach Hendricks' head as hard as he could, Mrs. Hendricks opened the door, and the light from the bedroom loomed Marty's shadow on the wall. Mrs. Hendricks screamed and Coach Hendricks turned and grabbed Marty's hand.

"Why, you little pigsqueak."

Marty's hand felt as if it was broken, each bone individually. The candlestick fell to the floor, and Mrs. Hendricks came out of her stupor, grabbed it up, and made as if she'd knock Marty out, but Coach Hendricks hit him with his right fist, and Marty doubled over feeling he'd never breathe normally again. Then before he hit the floor, the coach swung his left fist into his jaw.

That was when everything went black for Marty.

Chapter Twenty-Nine

Making money isn't hard in itself...What's hard is to earn it doing something worth devoting one's life to.

Carlos Ruiz Zafón

By the early part of the twenty-first century, improvements had been made in technology so that cell phones could send instant text messages, photographs, and videos around the world. Happenings in one hemisphere one minute could be seen in another hemisphere the next. But before telephone and telegraph, mental telepathy was sometimes used by people who cared a great about each other. Mental telepathy was the first *tele* and the first *pathy*; it was instilled by God to wire people of common focus in unexplainable ways and measures.

At the same time Marty was blacked out to the world, Blanche had a strong feeling something was not quite right. She tried telephoning him repeatedly but got no answer. She let the phone ring for as long as she could stand it, thinking he might be in the shower or had stepped out to his garage. No, something was wrong. At the same hour that Blanche was trying to call Marty, Doug had arrived into town—earlier than he had thought. He had canceled out on several stops because he had a weird feeling in his bones that fireworks were about to go off. He decided to detour by 501 and 378 and head to Marion by way of highway 908 that ran straight through Britton's Neck. He would call Marty and tell him to meet him at Williams' Restaurant for a cup of java and catch up on the events of Moe Lackey.

As he and his rig got closer, he couldn't get an answer so he decided to call Lukie at the Marion Police Department and tell him, "How 'bout meet me at Williams' to see what had been going down." And at the same time Doug was trying to call Lukie, Lukie had been covertly informed that Ken Hendricks had set up a tryst with a certain banker to post a predated document, which would transfer a huge chunk of the assets of the Davis Moe Lackey estate to the accounts of Ken Hendricks. Lukie had enlisted several other officers to assist him in making the arrest when the call came in from Doug.

"Doug, I can't talk right now. Things are happening tonight. I'll catch you tomorrow."

"Lukie, maybe that's why I'm having such strong vibes tonight about the Britton's Neck thing. I haven't been able to get Marty, and the last time we talked, he was planning to try to find who had kidnapped Mrs. Violet and her whereabouts."

"Whoa. Run that by me again."

"Yeah, he called to say that he wanted to try to get info from Mrs. Violet, but I told him to wait until I got back, and we'd go together. Tonight I've been trying to get him and can't. I just got this gut feeling that stubborn bastard is gonna try to get to the bottom of this on his own, and he's gonna get hurt. He said him and his aunt might try to find out something."

"Who is his aunt? Have you tried to reach her?"

"Blanche Fitzgibbons, a real nice lady. Maybe you could look up the number and give her a call."

"Will do. If you hear anything, give me a call back."

Luke kept getting a busy signal and began to feel relief that all was well. He still had an hour before the target time for the bust, so he called again. He owed a lot to Doug Dozier's old man. He had taught him the ropes at the police department when he came in from the Academy. He wouldn't want to leave any stone unturned in helping Alvin Dozier's son, Doug, and his other son Marty.

Blanche replaced the phone, lifted her eyes upward, and prayed a short, direct prayer, "Lord, please let Marty be okay." The phone rang. She jerked it up, expecting it to be Marty.

"Mrs. Fitzgibbons, this is Officer Luke Owens at the Marion Police Department. I'm a friend of Doug Dozier, and he's been trying to reach Marty Price. Is he there by any chance?"

"Oh, my Lord, Office Owens, is Marty all right? I'm worried out of my mind. I've been trying to reach him for hours. He left here determined to talk with Dr. Lackey. He should be home by now. I just know something has happened to him."

"Well, I tell you what, I'm going to make a routine check down that way. You sit tight and don't worry, ma'am. I'm sure your nephew is fine."

The other officers could make the arrest without his being present. He called Doug and told him he was leaving Marion and should arrive at his destination in fewer than fifteen minutes. His record was seven minutes.

Doug was waiting, and when he saw the police car, he

jumped up and met Luke in the parking lot. He got in the car with the young officer, and together they drove across the street and down the long driveway to the mansion. "That was Dr. Lackey's car behind his office, but there were no lights on in the office. And, I don't see any sign of Marty's Impala."

"Marty's shrewd, Lukie. He's sharper than a tack. He could've left his car somewhere else."

"Won't hurt to look around. Since we're here, that is."

Lukie drove up, and both men jumped out of the patrol car. No lights were on at the front door. They could see no lights on the inside. Lukie instinctively began walking around the house and motioned for Doug to go in the opposite direction. *These old plantation houses spook me out*, Doug thought. *I wouldn't live in one of 'em if my life depended on it. I'd rather live in one of these old tobacco barns.* "Oh, my goodness, there's the Impala!" He almost ran to it to see if Marty was in it.

By this time, Lukie had made his inspection and found that a light was on in the rear left room of the house. Then he saw Doug at the car. He motioned again for Doug to keep it quiet. They were on to something.

Doug wanted to burst in the house, but Lukie said they didn't have a search warrant even though things looked very suspicious. They went to the window that had the light and listened—nothing. Lukie went to his car phone and radioed that he might need a backup if one was available. He told them he'd wait ten minutes, and then they were going to enter the premises. He added, "Don't use the bells, okay? Keep it quiet."

Coach Hendricks had told his wife to give Marty one of

the same shots of the knock-out drug they'd been giving Moe. "He'll sleep until I get back, and by then we'll decide what to do with him. We might be able to make it look like he knocked out the doctor."

Marty had spent months in a coma in Korea. Now in his unconsciousness, he was back in Korea and could hear the voice of Captain Cecilia Seabrook. He imagined she was standing over him, her long reddish hair caught up in her military drab. She leaned over and was about to kiss his lips. He stirred. His entire body vibrated with a rush of warmth, he turned. Mrs. Hendricks had seen his movements and started toward the medicine kit that held the syringes and vials of drugs.

"Oh, no, you don't!" she shouted. Then Moe Lackey began to stir from the bed where they had placed him. "Oh, hell! Both of you. I'll take care of you both!" she screamed.

On the outside of the window, Doug heard the voice and listened, not knowing what she meant. He picked up one of the stones that were the line of demarcation of one of the plant arrangements around a tree. He flung it as accurately as he could toward the window.

"Damn, now what's that?" he heard her say from inside.

Doug hid as he saw her from above at the window. She pulled the draperies back, and he could clearly see the macabre face of Mrs. Hendricks in the window with the needle poised in her hand.

"Stop what you're doing and let us in," he yelled up at her. Then he ran to Luke.

"Hurry, you must break in. She's murdering them. I saw her in the window with a needle in her hand!"

Luke ran to the front door and beat on it for a few minutes then pulled his revolver and shot the lock. Together they ran toward the room. "Stay back," Luke warned Doug.

Luke still held his revolver as he forcefully entered the room. There stood Mrs. Hendricks with the needle poised in midair.

"Stop what you're doing, Mrs. Hendricks," Luke demanded.

"You come toward me, and I'll give him a shot that will kill him in ten seconds."

"Mrs. Hendricks, you don't want to do that. Put that needle down. NOW!"

"No, we've come too far. We are almost there. And you are not going to stop us. We're going to be rich for a change. Nothing is going to stop us."

Not being a veteran policeman, Lukie had dealt with drunks too drunk to stand up and robbers who were too scared to speak, but he'd had no experience in dealing with an intelligent person so motivated by greed that their senses were this distorted. "Mrs. Hendricks, you're a teacher. This is not you. You don't go around killing people. Now, please, put the needle down and walk around the bed and let's go get help for this man."

"No! I've slaved in this god-forsaken place for over forty years, and what has it got me? I'll tell you what—nothing! It's not right that some people get all the money and pleasure in life. It's not right, and some don't deserve it! Look at them—look! I'm going to kill them, and I'm going to kill you too if you try to stop me."

Doug was hearing every word from his concealment but

didn't know what he could do to help. It didn't seem as bad as it could be: One woman, one needle up against a police officer with a loaded gun and him.

"Mrs. Hendricks, maybe I should tell you something. The police have been onto your husband for some time now. We know he's been buying drugs. That's a criminal offense for which he'll go to prison, but the worse thing he's doing is having you murder Dr. Lackey. You think he plans to come back here to get you, don't you? We have been following his tracks all evening. We know where he is right this minute. He's on his way to the bank to cash in on the money he's stealing. And he's already made plans to fly out of Charlotte after midnight—alone."

Mrs. Hendricks shook her head and laughed incredulously. "That's a downright lie! He's coming back to help get rid of these bodies and then—"

"No, Mrs. Hendricks, we've already seen where he's bought one ticket out of Charlotte to Costa Rica. Did you apply for a passport recently? He did."

She stood on the other side of Dr. Lackey's prostrate body with the needle still in her hand, shaking her head from side to side as if she was trying to shake the truth away. She wasn't a murderer, really. She had been a coveter who had let her hunger for money erase all of her moral consciousness. Now it was too late. Her husband had enticed her by opening her eyes to forbidden fruit. She had shaken hands with the devil, and slowly but surely, he had consumed her. Her shoulders slumped under the weight of the devil's power. She looked at the full syringe in her hand. She had mixed the drug stronger than ever. No one could overcome this strength. She plunged it into her heart and left it there until she felt the flames rise up burning her with unbearable heat.

Luke spoke into his radio requesting an ambulance just as the assisting officer bound up the veranda steps and into the house and down the hall. Doug didn't say a word, just pointed toward the bedroom.

Chapter Thirty

You can be young without money,
but you can't be old without it.
Tennessee Williams

Marty awoke before the ambulance reached Marion Memorial Hospital and shifted his body to be able to see Moe on the gurney next to his. The medics were administrating an antidote to flush the deadly drug from Moe's body. Doug had called Blanche, and she was on the way to the hospital. Luke had stayed in Britton's Neck to wait for the crime lab people and coroner to take Mrs. Hendricks' body. He looked at the front door of the mansion and felt more than a tinge of guilt for having to shoot the lock. The solid brass lock was a perfect reminder of an earlier time in history reminiscent of refined living, but in the morning light, the refinement would not bring nostalgia, he thought, only ugliness.

Moe would spend a couple of days in the hospital for observation, but he would be fine. A doctor, younger than Moe, and one he'd met before, told him he had been given drugs for a long time in his food. He had "dodged the bullet" when all the stronger quantities of drugs were injected directly into his bloodstream. He could have been dead. The police also had explained what had happened when they brought him in by ambulance, but it was doubtful he would be able to understand and remember any of it.

The doctor had examined Marty, but Marty insisted he was fine—he'd survived worse in days gone by. He sat by Moe's bed. When Moe was alert, Marty had fits of talking, telling him he needed to hire an assistant doctor to help him, so he could take over the practice one day. He also needed a certified nurse who was not also the receptionist. After his bouts of chatter, Marty would then sit reticently as if rethinking all of his words.

When morning came Marty felt he needed to touch base with Doug and Luke. He and Doug met at the grill and then went together to the police department to talk to Luke. Marty told Luke all that had happened in Georgetown. He still had not mentioned to Moe about his mother.

Luke said he thought they needed to do something and not sit on it any longer. Part of the problem was over. The next part, hopefully, would turn out with no deaths—murders or suicides. "First, we must obtain a search warrant. And that's in Georgetown County. We'll have to play ball with those guys. I don't know if they know the rich doctor. We'd better be armed with lots of facts when we go down that road. You understand? That means we must question Moe about his knowledge of this Doctor Lackey."

The three of them sat in the small hospital room. The doctor who was on duty when Moe arrived by ambulance the night before came in also in case there were adverse effects from the interview. "You're doing much better today, Dr. Lackey. Apparently, some things were happening to you that you were not aware of, but don't worry about that. There will be no lasting consequences physically, I don't think. It is sad when people we trust turn out to be scoundrels, but it happens everyday. I'm sorry about the teacher. The policeman here, Officer Owens, needs to get some information from you. You feel up to it, sir?"

"Sure. But first, I think I need to apologize to Marty. I vaguely remember your being there last night. Where would I be without you, huh? Just, thanks."

Marty nodded and pointed to Doug, "This here is Doug, and he's really the one who hooked us up with the police. They're the ones to thank. They saved both our butts."

Moe acknowledged Doug, and Doug nodded back to him. He also reached out his hand to shake Doug's hand and then Luke's hand, "Thanks."

"Moe, I hope none of the questions will upset you. Some of the forms we need filled out can be done later, but one or two things I need to know today. And one of them concerns your mother."

"She's in the nursing home in Georgetown. That's where she wanted to go. But, to tell you the truth, I've not been back down to check on her. This business with the, you know— Is she doing okay? She doesn't know about the trouble last night, does she?"

"Well, Moe, let me just say that we don't know at present if she is safe or not. Now, the next question: Marty says he's never heard you mention your uncle in Georgetown, the one who is a doctor. Can you tell us something about him?" said Luke.

"There's nothing to tell. All I know is that my father had an older brother. I don't remember him. There are no more Lackeys that I know of. If he's a doctor, I didn't know it. My mother has never spoken of him. He's been living in a foreign country since I was a little boy," Moe said, pausing as if trying to search his memory.

"It seems he has been in Georgetown for a long time. Are you sure you've never heard your mother mention him?"

"I'm sure. She never discussed the family on either side. I know very little about any living relatives."

"Marty visited your mother at the nursing home to warn her about the Hendrickses. He was concerned they'd try to do something to her. It was a good thing too, because they did try to make contact with her. When Marty was with your mother, he asked her to elaborate on something she'd said about your late sister."

"Oh, what was that?" asked Moe.

Marty leaned toward the bed as far as possible. "Moe, the night the ambulance came for your mother, she had been drinking a lot and they'd—the Hendrickses—had given her drugs, but she said *she always thought they'd bring her back*. I don't think she was talking outta her head, and I wanted to ask her about it, so I went to see her at the nursing home. When I brought it up, she became hysterical, and they ran me outta the nursing home."

"After that, your friend here did quite a bit of detective work. He enlisted his aunt to go with him, but found your mother had disappeared from the nursing home. Plus, the doctor who was taking care of her was none other than Doctor Lackey. Since then, your mother and all her records seemed to have disappeared."

"My God! Are you telling me you don't know where she is?"

"Not yet. That's why we're asking you for all the information you can possibly give us. Maybe your mother has records at home. It gets a little bizarre, but Marty and his aunt did get a tip and found Doctor Lackey's home, and he admitted he had removed her from the nursing home for her own protection. But he wouldn't reveal where he's keeping her. We have a search warrant, and we're going to Georgetown. If you can add anything that would help us," Luke's voice trailed off as he studied Moe's perplexed expression.

"No, I don't know anything. I want to go with you."

"I'm afraid the strain would be a little too much for you right now, Dr. Lackey," said the doctor who had been observing Moe as Luke explained the situation.

"Don't worry, Moe. We'll find your mother and bring her back to Britton's Neck. Both of you should be as good as new, or better, in a few days." chimed in Marty.

Chapter Thirty-One

You can only become truly accomplished at something you love. Don't make money your goal.

Maya Angelou

Luke pulled out the search warrant and showed it to the maid, who stepped back from the door and immediately went to the telephone. The officers began going from room to room, turning up anything that was turned down and opening doors and drawers. Luke asked if the doctor was at home and was told he was at the nursing home.

"Back here," one of the officers yelled. Luke quickly walked to a room located off from a large bedroom. The room was smaller but furnished nicely in all white and gold: a gold bed with white pillows and spread, white shag carpet, white loveseat and recliner with gold throw pillows, white plant stands with ferns, large prints of white water egrets in gold frames, gold lamps with white shades, flowing white curtains, and white ceiling fan above. Off from that bedroom was a full bathroom. "Here are items that are likely to belong to Mrs. Lackey—that is, Mrs. Violet Lackey. They're monogrammed with her initials *VL*. Here's a woman's silk robe, also monogrammed *VL*."

"But where is she?"

"Here are ladies clothes in the closet."

Luke walked over to examine the closet: Dozens of pairs of shoes. Dozens of dresses. A fur coat in a zippered bag. Expensive handbags on a top shelf along with beach hats. He pulled one of the dresses from the closet. "What size woman is Mrs. Lackey? Most of these dresses don't look like something an older woman would wear. Plus, these dresses are," he looked at a label, "size four. Do you think Mrs. Violet is that small?"

"You're right. My wife looked at one like that in Saks when we were down at Hilton Head. Whew! Needless to say, on my salary, she didn't get it."

"I think it's about time we locate and talk to this Doctor Lackey," said Luke.

Luke tried to question the maid, but she refused to say anything. He left one of his men at the house and took the other along with him to the nursing home. He showed his badge and asked for Doctor Lackey. The receptionist stood and said quietly, "Follow me."

She led the officers through the nursing chatter and the awkward reaching out of a few of the wheelchair patients who seemed to recognize someone from their past. Luke looked sympathetic but tried not to make eye contact. Some patients were sitting in an alcove with visitors trying to visit and carry on a conversation. Luke followed the receptionist down one winding hallway after another until they came to closed double doors marked NO ENTRY. She pushed the electronic plate on the wall and waited a few moments before pushing open the door. They entered a hallway very unlike the rest of the facility. The halls were not as brightly lit and there seemed to be no windows. Only one nurse sat at a desk.

They continued walking and turning down another hallway. Finally, the receptionist stopped before one of the doors and stood aside.

Luke pushed the door slightly and then more, so that he could see. The room was dark. He reached to turn on the light. "No, don't do that! Please! Don't turn on that light," came a heavy voice from the center of the room.

"Doctor Lackey?"

"Yes."

"I need to ask you some questions."

Gradually the room appeared to allow light, and Luke pushed the door open to be able to see that a woman lay on the bed, and Doctor Lackey sat in a chair as close to the bed as possible with his head lying on the body of the woman. His shoulders were heaving, but no sound came from his mouth.

As Luke continued to observe, he knew the woman was dead. Her head was placed on soft, downy pillows. Her graying golden hair spread over the pillows to make her look peacefully asleep. Her arms were down by her sides as if she were waiting for a lover. She was dressed in a flowing nightgown of shimmering white silk with the initials *VL* stitched in soft gold on the left breast.

Luke stood respectfully quiet for several more minutes. The silent crying did not let up. "Doctor Lackey, is this woman Violet Lackey? When did she die?"

For the first time, his mournful wails filled the room. "Yes, it is Violet. Yes, it is she. Yes, yes, yes."

He lifted his distorted face, and Luke could see it was wet with his tears. He lifted one of her hands and kissed it and rubbed the tears on his face and then kissed the hand again. Luke spoke again, "How long has she been dead, Doctor Lackey?"

"What difference does it make? What difference does it make? She's been dead to me all my life. I've only had her for an instant. Just an instant. Such an instant." His shoulders shook again with silent grief.

Chapter Thirty-Two

Money is usually attracted, not pursued.

Jim Rohn

Doctor Lackey began, "He was supposed to get her *for me*. I saw her first. I saw her at the Democratic Convention at the Jefferson Hotel in Columbia. She was with her daddy. She was sixteen and the most beautiful creature I'd ever seen. I couldn't take my eyes off her. I knew she would never look at me. My brother Davis was the one who was smooth and debonair and knew how to talk to the ladies, and he had the manners. He made an art out of it. He was also trying to get into politics. I gave him half of my inheritance to win her over for me.

"But instead of winning her for me, he won her for himself. He was smitten, like me, with her fair skin and sparkling blue eyes. It was like looking into the Atlantic Ocean on a sunny day just looking into those eyes. And her hair was all kinds of golden. She was all the princesses in all the nursery rhymes and all the goddesses in all the myths that were ever written or told. My heart ached within my body to even think of her. I trembled when I thought of even speaking to her. If she had called my name, I would have broken out completely in body perspiration. I was twenty-two and an utter fool over her. I would have sold my soul to the devil for her. I would have given half my life for her. In fact, that is exactly what I did. I sold my soul to the devil, and I did give half my life, for I trusted my brother.

"But he," his eyes grew cold and his chin trembled and turned to stone. His hand went up and shook in the air. "But he, my very own brother, whom I trusted with everything, he won her to himself. I doubt he ever mentioned my name to her. He came back to Georgetown from Columbia and said, 'Her father will never let her go. I must do something drastic.' And I asked him, 'What do you mean? Did you tell him we have money? Did you tell him we have power, just like he does?' 'Her father isn't interested in how wealthy or how powerful we are. He called me a lowcountry half-breed. He said I was never to approach his daughter again, and if I did, it would cost more than I wanted to pay—it would cost me my life.'

"So my brother, I knew, had not even mentioned my name. He had introduced himself as a possible suitor for Violet and left me out entirely. He took my inheritance. He took my youth, for I could never have loved another like I loved Violet. His valiant display before her father caused her to fall in love with him. Nothing makes a young girl love more than the knowledge she is loved by someone forbidden. Davis Lackey was the forbidden fruit for this perfect Eve. She had to taste the one thing in her entire life that was being withheld—Davis. Then that caused her to become the forbidden fruit for me. I had to live in agony each and every day of my young life just knowing my brother enjoyed what I cherished more than the very air I breathed, more than my own life. This was to be my fate.

"I couldn't bare to see them. I forced my parents to exclude him from our home by telling them I'd take my own life if I had to see them together. I left for Europe and was gone for a couple of years. During that time, her father ruined it for him in politics, made it impossible for Davis to get elected to any office—national, statewide, even local. He never had a chance after he took Violet. They found the old plantation house in Britton's Neck, far enough away and so isolated that they could make a life there. They still came once a month to worship. When I returned from Europe, I stayed in the shadows. Seeing her was unbearable for me.

"She never dreamed in a million years that her family would disown her if she married Davis. That was like a whip upon her lovely back. She couldn't bare the loneliness. She shut herself off from everyone out of her despair for her father and mother and cousins she had been so close to during her childhood in Columbia and the upstate. They, however, would not forgive her. They were a proud people. Can you imagine giving up the treasure of the world?"

He turned toward the stonelike body on the pillows, letting his fingers sweep across her face. He gently lifted a strand of the long hair and brought it to his lips and kissed it passionately.

"And then she birthed her very likeness—Hazeline. My heart began to breathe again as I watched Hazeline. She would be more to me than Violet because I would own her from her birth—I'd own every minute of her life. From the shadows, I watched her. I studied her when they'd come to Georgetown. I worshipped her. I knew she would be mine. She would fulfill the emptiness of my heart that had been left by Violet. She was the treasure of my heart.

"So when she became the age that Violet had been when I fell so desperately in love with her, I claimed her. I stole her. I enticed her to come to me under the guise of my taking her to the operetta. I had someone I trusted bring her to Conway. She wondered why I didn't want her parents to know, but so innocent was she, she didn't question me, and I picked her up, but instead of going to Georgetown, we headed for the coast of Florida. She still didn't question me, and my hands trembled so on the steering wheel, I could hardly drive. When she was hungry, we stopped for food, but I couldn't eat. My nervousness ate away my appetite as it had eaten away my caution. My love for her was more than I was. My love was greater than all humanity.

"You may think I sound like a eccentric schoolboy, but I tell you, it is true. A starved heart can grow bold and reckless. As we drove all day toward the Keys, I wanted to hold her to me and caress her as I had longed for years to hold and caress Violet. All her life, I'd dreamed of her belonging to me. As she grew and filled out to be a woman, I fantasized that I was touching her but never would have lost control. She was only a child, and I was an adult. But now she had become a full woman, with a woman's body and a woman's mind and a woman's capacity to love in return. The thought had never occurred to me that she wouldn't love me back in the same way I loved her, but on the drive to Florida, the thought did occur. What would happen to my injured psyche if she refused me? If she turned away from me to go to someone else as her mother had done?

"As she drove up to a roadside motel for the evening,

she turned to me so sweetly and said, 'Uncle, are we staying tonight in this place? I rather like the idea of the adventure.' Did I tell you that she had a brilliant mind? In that category, she far exceeded her mother. And it came to me, that her love for me might not come as directly as mine for her. I might need to use my wits to capture her physical love through her intellect. All her life I'd doted on how smart she was growing. I was a doctor, and she would become a lady doctor—not a nurse as people expected women to be. Or a scientist—she had the brain to become a scientist. My only doubt was my own feelings. I wasn't sure I could control myself another day. I wasn't sure I could lie in the same room, breathe the same air, smell her, hear her minute murmurs and sighs, and not explode with passion so powerful that I could destroy all hope that she would come to me voluntarily."

He hung his head as if what he had to tell was too sorrowful for tears. Maybe his tears had already been spent a million times over.

"Go on, Dr. Lackey," said Officer Luke.

"I cannot."

"What happened to Hazeline, Doctor? Where is she now?"

"She was so innocent around me. She could see straight through others. Her eyes held the same magic as her mother's—they could stop a train. I trembled many times just looking into those blue eyes. I took our little luggage into the motel room, and she announced that she would not sleep closest to the door—that I was to have that bed. So I decided since she was exhausted from the long drive, I would force myself to sleep. Besides, we would have the rest of our lives together.

"The following day I awoke to find she had made a list of things she wanted to do and see while we were together on this adventure. I couldn't very well tell her of my intentions—that I wanted her as my wife.

"We boarded a boat to Cuba. And from there, we went on to see the world—as many places as we could without being in direct connection to the war. Many people thought she was my daughter, and I never said yay nor nay to stupid remarks made by stupid people. And she never answered them either. She was able to study medicine in Switzerland with the very best doctors in the world. She trusted me, and I loved her and gave her everything. I made her think her family had disowned her and refused to see her again. Of course, she cried at times for her mother and father and brother, but I forced her to turn her grief into creative endeavors. Our families had never displayed serious binding connections, so she grew to accept that as fact.

"My lawyers had started the nursing home even before we arrived back in Georgetown. My parents were gone by then. Davis had died. Both of us were eager to begin the nursing home. It occupied our days and nights. I was learning to transfer all my passions for Hazeline to the work of the nursing home. People were loyal to me beyond the call of duty.

"At home, she slept in a room where I could slip in during the night and gaze at her sleeping. I know you think I'm insane. Ours was a divine love. I grew to acknowledge that I would never have her as a wife in the physical sense; nevertheless, she was my soul mate. She worked frantically hard, but she started drinking hard as well. She became a chain smoker when she was not with patients. I had to medicate her for her to be able to sleep.

"It is odd how the gods played with me. I knew they were using me for a toy when Hazeline became ill—too ill to work. At first she took a bed at the nursing home and worked from there, but gradually her mind started going. All of the medical knowledge and technology in the world and none could save her. Nothing could save her. I couldn't save her. I had the carpenters seal off her room, in fact, the entire hall.

"And then almost on cue—Violet showed up at the hospital by ambulance from Marion Memorial Hospital. In the same week that Hazeline died, Violet returned, can you imagine? We put her in her very own room, and she was thriving beyond belief. All the powers in the world could not hold back the resurgence of passion I held for her. Even after all this time. Age had not diminished her immense beauty; age had made her all the more desirable to me. My soul had burned for her once; now it burned even more for her again. She didn't recognize me when I first went to her room. And then I told her who I was. She remembered then. She had always strongly suspected there was a connection to Hazeline's disappearance and our family, but it was too inconceivable to be thought true. Just like she had thought her family would never disown her. Her innocent mind could not maneuver injustice and pain. Like mother, like daughter—neither of them could see evil in me. And it wasn't evil. It was having what was mine! And just as I'd convinced her of my sympathies and loyalties, while my hopes were starting to blossom again, Marty Price showed up and then the couple showed up asking for her. I had to move her out of the hospital.

"I had to let her know how Davis had tricked me. He

had stolen her from her parents, and he had stolen her from me. When I told her, she became hysterical. She knew then that Hazeline had gone with me, but she didn't know why Davis wouldn't try to find her. Now she thought I had only been avenging myself by stealing Hazeline. She couldn't understand how I didn't see it as stealing. It was my unrequited love for her that had transferred to Hazeline.

"Violet wanted to know where Hazeline had been all these years. I took her to Hazeline's old room, so that it could become her room now. All would have been well, had not Martin Price and his aunt come looking for her. She would have grown to love me. She had to have loved me sooner of later. I loved her enough for both of us.

"After their appearance, I had to move her back here to the nursing home. I wanted her more than life, but she shuttered when I went near her. You must understand; I had to have her. I'd wanted her and had waited all my life for her love. I had to have her—my life of longing—*I had to have her*. I'd often given Hazeline a tranquilizer to help her sleep. In fact, she'd gotten used to them, but I never could bring myself to make love to her even sedated—she was so young, so pure, so holy. She had become a goddess that I worshipped.

"I had to have Violet. I gave her a tranquilizer as I had done Hazeline to make her sleep just so I could gaze upon her beauty. I thought a tranquilizer might make it easier for Violet since she had been ill. But then I couldn't bear to wait for a drug to take effect. I didn't think she would resist me. I wanted her to feel my love, to know how much a lifetime of cherishing had built up inside me. I knew she would feel my love and give me her love in return. When I began to kiss her and fondle her, she fought me. But I could not stop. Now that she was here in the flesh, not a dream any longer, I could not stop the avalanche of love inside me."

He pulled her robe closer together and reached up to touch her lips with his long, thin fingertips.

"She fainted. I could not stop loving her."

Again he put his head down.

"And then you came."

Chapter Thirty-Three

You cannot serve God and money.

Matthew 6:24 (ESV)

"You know I ain't gifted with words. Never have been. And I ain't capable of putting it in just the right words. *Mot juste*." Marty looked away as if he were trying to see a certain person.

"When I was in the Army there was this red-headed nurse—she told me that *mot juste* is what the French call finding just the right words for saying something. I liked that expression—*mot juste*. Most of the time, it's too complex for me—life—that is. The words to describe life slip in and out of my mind like a memory of a rainbow. You know, you've seen it and one day, you hope you'll see it again because it's so like a little bit of heaven slipping through the clouds, but you can't actually describe it like it really is. There's no *mot juste* for me to say what I'm about to try to say, hear? This is about as close as I can get."

Moe shoved his chair back, scraping the floor with a nerve-racking screech.

Marty, in his discombobulated tone, continued, "Listen, you'd think that the higher you get to the top, the more you have to see, but, actually, the higher you get to the top *the less* you actually see. Understand? I guess like climbing Mount

Everest would be. Many people start out to climb, but most of them give up the climb as the mountain gets steeper. There's less to see as you climb up the mountain."

"Rainbows! Mount Everest! What in the devil has gotten into you, Marty? What are you talking about?"

"Life." He paused and their eyes never touched though both men were looking intently into the past, present, and future of their lives. "I am putting together something, and I need to tell you before it slips away again. These few things seem to add up to being my life. Hear me out, okay?

"First of all, it seems some people are born good, and they are good, and they do good, and only once in awhile they deviate from that path, see? But when they do, they can't bear it until they get matters straightened out, undo the harm they've caused—fix the situation in some way—like I would fix up a messed-up car engine. But those people are one in a million. They only come a few to each generation, you know, the people who can really fix things for everybody else.

"But then, there are the rest of us. We were born bad, and we do bad without thinking twice about it. It is natural for us to just be bad. Once in a while we may let our conscious nag us, but only if someone jumpstarts our conscious. Our conscious is, uh, like it's *asleep*, you see? Someone must point out and plead for us to see our badness. Like that preacher at the tent meeting that time when we were kids. Like Aunt Blanche does in an underhanded way— (I don't mean underhanded in a bad way, understand?) If she does something, it can't be bad in any way.

"Getting back to my point, even if someone who's bad is talked into feeling guilty, it's only for a little while. We may have genuine remorse but only for a split second. Then it's back to business as usual, being bad. And that one time back when we were at that tent meeting, remember? For a moment after that, it was like a little light glowing and getting bigger. I could see something I'd never seen or understood before. That thing about Jesus' blood is thick enough to cover the bad and hide it from God's eyes. Just for a while the world here in Britton's Neck and all over the world seemed to be in focus and balanced—like *mot juste*—when you find the exact word you want to use to describe something. How I saw life—all of life—that had a meaning and a reason and a… hope.

"Moe, I'd like to think that life does have a meaning. You've been through as much hell as me and as anyone else, but there's still a meaning for it all.

"Way back then, I saw that little glimmer, and I believed it. Then going to Korea and what happened there, it got pushed way back in my mind. When mama died, I saw how she had spent her whole life for nothing but for me. She only gave—she never took. Even in her dying, she gave me my father. Then I was able to find him and a brother I never knew existed. It's a good feeling, Moe, a damn good feeling. I don't want to let it go, and I hope I'll get more of it before I die."

Moe Lackey sat listening to his corncob friend who was talking more than he ever had. Who knows, Marty might have just said more than he'd ever said his entire life. He himself became reflective. Both of them had been born under a curse. Marty's curse was broken when his mother Pauline Price died. Yes, Moe thought, that is exactly when Marty began to change. Marty cut ties to him and went searching for his father and found him and a brother as well.

Moe realized he, himself, had never gone searching for anyone. He had never searched for his sister. He'd never searched to find out more about his parents' families. He'd only stumbled upon his mother's people's existence. He'd never tried to understand her or her former life. He'd only used her as he had used all the people in his life for his own interest. He'd neglected forming friendships, and the few he'd had—like with Marty—he'd twisted and abused. Was there hope he could break the curse? Would he ever be able to love anyone like his uncle had? Even without having his love returned, his uncle had loved more passionately in his lifetime than most people could possible imagine.

He realized that Marty had found something genuine—something holy, beyond himself. What Marty was trying to articulate was God—Marty had found—or was putting the pieces together to find God, for surely there is a God of the Universe who breaks curses.

The End